Stephanie Olds

THE WOUNDS
THAT ENDURE

The Wounds That Endure by Stephanie Olds

Printed in the United States of America
First Edition—Second Printing, May 2025
ISBN: 978-1968178017

Ink and Revival Publishing
Virginia, USA

"To every single person who has ever found themselves in a dark place, but regained enough strength to rise above the pain, I celebrate you.

And to every single person who continues to stand tall with all their blemished broken pieces held together by faith, I celebrate you.

You are strong — Stay strong!"

Stephanie Olds

TABLE OF CONTENTS

PROLOGUE

UP AGAINST IT

"Anything that's human is mentionable, and anything that is mentionable can be more manageable. When we can talk about our feelings, they become less overwhelming, less upsetting, and less scary. The people we trust with that important talk can help us know that we are not alone."
— *Fred Rogers*

I want to be dead. Nowadays more than ever. I always thought that life would be rewarding and reciprocal, where doing good things and being a good person would provide a sense of return, a personalized gratification. I thought life would always respond to my positive action with another positive action, a kind enriching action.

On the eve of my 40th birthday, I'm taking the time to reflect and finally acknowledge to myself that this is not how life works. For several months now, I have reached out to the people who are closest to me, my people, my friends, presenting them with the once-in-a-lifetime opportunity to celebrate my 40th birthday with me. My suggestions and ideas for memorializing the milestone were met with explanations and justifications for why each couldn't be in attendance on that day, or at that time.

Sad to say, desertion is something I've long been familiar with, though I've never had the luxury of getting accustomed to. Despite being acquainted with, somehow, I still take it personally and permit it to be a poison to my spirit. Throughout my life, I've been courteous and kindhearted, helpful to one and all, yet when it comes down to planning a social gathering to celebrate me, no one cares to participate. This is typical.

As a matter of fact, I can hardly remember the celebrations of my childhood because, truthfully, celebration wasn't a priority for us. We did acknowledge things like birthdays with a cake and some ice cream. That was a wonderful treat, but a real, authentic party or festival was extremely rare.

I was brought up supposing that a real celebration comes at the end of work. This idea came from generations of people who knew that they couldn't afford to let their guards down because not being vigilant could result in their untimely death. This innate sense of fear is what I think to be the primary reason why I struggle with celebration in my own life.

Even though I have been successful and accomplished, I'm always anxious about losing what I have, so I never really stop to celebrate. I have resolved to categorize it as a subconscious way for me to protect myself. My rationale is if I let my guard down and fully enjoy something, then I might experience more pain if I lose it. So, I try to maintain control by not allowing my joy to make me vulnerable like this.

The saddest part is that I am just now realizing this tonight. Half a lifetime complete and I'm finally understanding and accepting the actuality that honestly, the work is never finished. There's always something more to be achieved. So, celebration keeps fleeing into the future, never to be experienced.

For the first time, I am able to see what I've done. All my life I've been depriving myself of joy and replacing it with fear.

Glancing over my left shoulder I set my eyes on a little rabbit, hopping away into the distance quickly. I have wild rabbits in my backyard. They love to show their wonderful faces mostly during the spring and summer. This year has been a little different because I haven't seen them much at all. I have seen at least one of them about once or twice a week when I take my dog Cheddar out before bed. This is way less than I've seen them other years.

My rabbits prefer to have the sunflower seeds and kale. Here in Chattanooga, the summers are very warm and that can make feeding, even at night, difficult. I've tried leaving several other options out but over time I learned that they prefer the sunflower seeds and the kale the most.

Refocusing, I begin to thoughtfully consider my wins. I'm questioning has fear really controlled my life? Optimistic, I embark on a new line of thinking, beginning by readily admitting to myself several truths that one would think might invoke instant happiness.

I recognize that accomplishing the goals you set can be a very rewarding experience.

It's not that I didn't know this previously. No, I've been aware most of my life. Thankfully, with the consistent nurturing and supportive guidance from my grandma, I learned this early on. She instilled in us that goal setting is a process. It starts with careful consideration of what you want to achieve and ends with a lot of hard work to actually do it.

"Reachin' ya goals is one of da greatess thangs you'ca do fo' yo'sef ", is what grandma said.

Admitting it now is necessary for me because I always needed more to go with accomplishing the goal. I needed accolades. Despite what grandma said, I needed to know that someone else was proud of me for my achievements. Someone besides me.

Now, I'm allowing myself to acknowledge that the praise and honor are my personal responsibility. I set goals that motivate me. I aim to achieve certain objectives because they are important to me. It's always imperative that *I* see value in the things that I strive for, so why then does it matter if someone else recognizes my hard work and dedication? Tonight, as I sit on my patio reflecting on my life, I finally acknowledge that it *doesn't* matter, and it never did.

CHAPTER ONE

THE DEEP SOUTH

"It is easier to build strong children than to repair broken men."
— *Frederick Douglass*

I grew up in a small town called Fort Le Coeur. A very unique community with a population of only about 1,900 people, Fort Le Coeur provided me with the social foundations, strength and resilience that I would need to reach my goals.

As fate would have it, the literal meaning of Forte Le Coeur was "Strong Heart". A predominantly African American community kinda on the Mississippi River, our town was made of an industrious people, all striving to make a better life for their ménage. Growing up, I would always see my parents, neighbors and fellow townsfolk all working energetically and devotedly to provide for their families. The tenacity of the community was something to really be proud of.

Though steady work was available, there weren't many options to choose from. The labor market in our area was a peculiar one due primarily to the location.

Forte Le Coeur was about 9 miles away from the river and about

79 miles north of the metropolis. We lived in the country, which was not close to any large cities, but also conveniently positioned on the main transportation routes between New Orleans and Chicago.

We shared schools with another nearby town, Tulip, but *nearby* was 15 miles away. One amusing memory I have of our town is how rare vehicles were. You could always count on there being just one car of a particular make, model, and color per person. One thing was always certain—you might not recognize the driver, but you would definitely know who owned that car!

Forte Le Coeur started as a lumber mill town but is now completely supported by the agriculture industry. Sitting up around the fireplace in the wintertime, I remember how my grandma used to tell us of how Forte Le Coeur came to be:

She said, *"...ya'll have so much opportunities deese days an'yu jus squanda'um. Back when I was comin' up, you was boan in da company, you worked fo' da company, you woe company clothes, you ate company food, an' you died in da company. What I knowed as opportunities was mostly jus work camps. Limit'd conditions, you had a place to sleep an' den of corse you had da commissary stoe. Dat didn't matter much doe, da prices was all sky high! Da mens was paid in company notes, company scripts an' dat money wasn't no good anyplace else beside the commissary."*

Grandma told us how she and my grandpa left a different camp with a handful of other black families who were fleeing lynchings, and other racial horrors, to found Forte Le Coeur.

At the time she said that a new lumber mill was being built in Charles County. At first, everyone was excited about it. The mill was going to be capable of producing 250,000 board feet of lumber per day. Usually, when all the wood in the area had been cut, the town and mill were dismantled and moved to a new location. But this time, when the mill left, the town stayed.

"Folks got tied'a da man comin in, destroyin' an leavin'. Da towns was neva meant to be permanen...onliss lassin round bout a yea or two. We jus soon got tied'a movin' , tied a bein like slaves. An' good thing we did get tied 'cause you know evenchlly da most of lumber companies soon went unda."

To sustain, Forte Le Coeur took advantage of the newly cleared land. They started with one mule, two chickens, a goat and a handkerchief full of corn seeds. They worked hard and found progress in bartering with people in other settlements, but mostly in Tulip. Building on faith and stealing opportunities, they soon created a strong future.

As agricultural workers, a large majority of the people there took work to maintain crops and tend to livestock. To this day it's still the same. Some people perform physical labor while others operate machinery under the supervision of farmers, ranchers, and other agricultural managers.

While anyone you meet will tell you that they have their own business, this isn't the case. They typically work for someone as an equipment operator, animal breeder, greenhouse laborer or a ranch animal farm worker. Almost all available income is gained by harvesting and inspecting crops by hand, irrigating farm soil and maintaining ditches. Some work with pipes and pumps, stuff that keeps other stuff going. They operate and service farm machinery and tools, spray fertilizer or pesticide solutions to control insects, fungi, and weeds.

Plenty of the younger folk start out with light work moving shrubs, plants, and trees with wheelbarrows. They usually promote to using tractors, feeding livestock and cleaning and disinfecting their pens, cages, and yards once they get a little older.

Some people who have been to the university might be working to examine animals to detect symptoms of illnesses or injuries and administer vaccines to protect animals from disease. The school teaches them how to use brands, tags, or tattoos to mark livestock in order to identify ownership and grade. A couple of muscle-bound guys can be found herding livestock to pastures for grazing or to scales, trucks, or other enclosures.

Only a handful of the strongest entrepreneurial minds actually own a business in Forte Le Coeur. Other than that, people are able to find work on the docks as stevedores and longshoreman, but that work pays well and is much more difficult to get into. Somehow there are a few, now less than 10 people in the community, who have been able to find work at a chemical plant down closer to the city.

In Forte Le Coeur, the population count has been stagnant for some time. Most people realize the town needs to grow and attract more business somehow. In true political fashion, the local council says they are working on it, but many are cynical about this as previous efforts were fruitless. The truth is, politics around there always felt like a game of smoke and mirrors— promises made but rarely kept. It was hard to trust the words of politicians when their actions always seemed to benefit their own agendas more than the community. People learned the hard way that the council's priorities rarely aligned with the needs of the town—just another round of empty rhetoric while the rest of us kept waiting for change.

So, with job choices somewhat limited, a lot of the kids finish high school, leave town to go to a university in a big city and only come back to visit after that.

I left.

For me, I hated for the longest time the fact that we lived in a small town where everyone knew everyone else. I was dismayed that there weren't any fancy restaurants we could frequent, and that there was a myriad of activities that we had heard of on TV but could not pursue.

For nine years, I could grudgingly taste the dusty air in my mouth on our routine rides to school on the dirty bumpy roads that almost always reeked of cow-shit. When I was promoted to the middle school, I was a diligent student, but I longed for freedom even when I barely had an idea of what the word meant.

I grew up feeling lonely, restless, trapped, and agitated. I couldn't understand my parents' painstaking attempts at making my childhood a memorable one. Perpetually, I wanted to get away from everyone and everything.

Viola

Habitually, my grandma spoke in kind. Her good-natured, warm, selfless and accommodating character was my first introduction to loving others as God first loved us. Being a faithful example of what it means to offer love to all; she was the one that planted the seed of hope in me. With only a second-grade education, she cared for others and encouraged their individual growth and development in a manner that I have never seen in anyone else. On no account was there ever a chance that you would go without—a meal, a bed, a whipping, a hug—if Momo was near.

No struggle would be endured alone because grandma was

brave, and she intentionally shared her love with all who crossed her path.

From a very young age of around two years old, I can remember seeing my grandma prioritize the needs and necessities of those around her. She was very consistent and always put others before herself.

Sometimes, when we were getting on towards the end of the month she would make us breakfast with fried eggs and old, leftover rice. It was always so good, especially if she had cut up a hot dog wiener in it! She would make up our plates and call us to the table. If any of us asked why she was only drinking coffee and not eating with us, she would say it was because she wasn't hungry. It took me until I was about 8 years old to calculate the truth. Grandma was sacrificing to make sure there was enough food to go around to us three kids.

In her lifetime, she raised over 50 foster children and that is a testament to her humility. She embodied the Christian ideal of compassion, kindness, gentleness and patience.

This lady had an angelic presence. She was short and slim, her flawless skin a sepia, reddish brown color. As long as I'd known her, she was textbook beautiful with taut skin that was healthy, smooth, and fresh. Her salt and pepper hair was usually bound in a thick braid cascading down her back.

Only five feet tall, she was not just physically beautiful, she was beautiful from her heart and soul. Grandma made the space around her beautiful too. She affected others and brought their beauty out of them. She seemed to wrap her arms around the world, and she did it with ease, because it was just who she was.

Born in 1919, her gift was helping others to love themselves. She taught us things we could not learn from a schoolbook—virtues and lessons that were to remind us to remember our wholeness, remember what we deserved, remember our worth, remember the value we bring, remember self-compassion, remember self-care and self-love.

She would say, *"Rememba to consistently ress, replenish, an' refuel yo'sef. Rememba you is enough as you are. Rememba yo' power."*

The flower that made others bloom, she elevated herself with both her attitude and the way she loved with complete strength.

Up until her passing two years ago, just about all of the living previous foster dependents maintained contact with my grandma. Even if it was only to call and say "Merry Christmas" or to stop by the house and sing happy birthday.

There were two or three of her foster children that were still a close part of the family well after I was born. One in particular was nicknamed Black. He was close to the family because he didn't have any other relatives around. Black was in jail a lot and grandma was always the first person that he called. She would rotate her responses, depending upon the charge. Sometimes she would bail him out right away but other times she would have him stay in there to serve out his time. Black wasn't a violent man, though he did have two sticky hands.

Still but a kid, I distinctly remember the rumbling and ruckus that occurred in our house one night. It was a crisp autumn night when Black, at the ripe age of 30, found himself in a predicament that would be the talk of family gatherings for years to come. The moon hung low and full, casting a silvery glow over the quiet neighborhood, as Black, in a state of questionable sobriety, decided that he was in dire need of a midnight snack. Now, the thing about Black—and this is where his life gets interesting—is that he had a bit of a problem with crack cocaine. It wasn't the "good ol' days of youthful rebellion" kind of problem, but more like a "I-just-ate-an-elephant's-worth-of-candy-and- now-I-can't-sit-still" kind of problem. He'd tried to kick it several times, but the addiction was like that one relative who wouldn't leave at Thanksgiving—always there, lurking in the corner, grinning like it knew something you didn't. Hungry and intoxicated, his good decision-making skills were not on duty, which led him to the most logical action: go to the elementary school cafeteria.

Now, Black wasn't a man of half-measures. If he was going to break into a cafeteria, he was going to do it with style. Armed with nothing but a fork he had found in his jacket pocket and a determination fueled by questionable substances, he made his way to the school.

The lock on the cafeteria door was no match for his ingenuity—or rather, his ability to find an open window around the back.

Once inside, Black was like a kid in a candy store, if the candy store were filled with industrial-sized cans of baked beans and an inexplicable amount of Jell-O. He got to work, creating what could only be described as a culinary masterpiece, or a disaster, depending on your perspective. He mixed spaghetti with chocolate pudding, topped it with a generous helping of shredded cheese, and called it "Spaghettipuddeluxe."

As he sat there, fork in hand, sampling his creation with the gusto of a Michelin-star chef, the flashing red and blue lights outside went unnoticed. The police, alerted by a silent alarm, arrived in record time. They found Black sitting proudly at the lowest, kid-sized table in the cafeteria, surrounded by a buffet of his own making, humming a tune that sounded suspiciously like "Jingle Bells."

When the officers knocked on the locked cafeteria door, Black, in his infinite wisdom, decided it was only polite to let them in. He stumbled to the door, fork still in hand, and greeted them with a wide grin. *"Evening, ossifers!"*, while extending his arm to welcome them inside. *"Hungry? It's plenty and it's free!"*.

The officers, trying to maintain their composure, politely declined. They couldn't help but chuckle at the absurdity of the situation. Here was a man, clearly out of his mind, offering them a highly illegal meal that looked like it had been concocted by a toddler left unsupervised in a kitchen.

As they gently escorted Black to the squad car, he continued to extol the virtues of his culinary creation, insisting that they were making a bad mistake by not eating anything. The officers nodded along, trying to suppress their laughter as they loaded him into the back seat.

The next morning, Black found himself in a familiar setting: the county jail. As he sat there, nursing a headache that felt like a marching band had taken up residence in his skull, he realized he had one phone call. Naturally, he called my grandma.

Growing up, he always thought that he was smarter than everyone else. He was good at doing magic tricks and telling lies. A natural born con artist who would do anything to get over.

As he got older, grandma said, when people became hip to his schemes, he graduated to just plain old taking what he wanted. A thief. A liar. A jailbird.

But in the words of Viola:

"Git rid of arrogant from your heart. Don'chu eva look down on anotha no matta how less well-off dey might be. Rememba, da ones you look down on taday might be da same person you

have 'ta look up 'ta damorrow. "

Grandma was full of wisdom and life quotes to live by. She shared so many of her memories with us and made sure we had them etched in our brains. Honestly, for many years there wasn't much else to do in terms of entertainment, so we were blessed to have her.

I've heard so many stories about her sending someone up to the filling station to buy a gallon of coal oil. I'm still tickled by how I used to be so confused because I was not sure if she was saying "coal oil" or "cold oil"!

My grandmother, with her weathered hands and sharp eyes that held the wisdom of decades, used to share stories of her youth with us, stories that seemed almost too tough to be true. She would speak of a time when hardships were a constant companion, and perseverance was the only option. But the one story that stayed with me more than any other was the one she talked about being pregnant with my uncle while still having to work in the sugar cane fields.

It was one of those evenings when the house was alive with the familiar sounds of my grandmother's soft chuckle and the rhythmic whir of the evening breeze passing through the open window. We had gathered in the living room, me sitting at her feet as usual, listening intently as she began her story, her voice warm yet tinged with a kind of rawness that spoke volumes about the years she had lived through.

"I rememba bein' pregnan wit yo' unca," she started, *"an' da weatha was already gettin' hot, da cane was ready fo' harvest, an' dere weren't no stoppin'. No way of ascapin' dat work. Da sun beat down on me like it ain't had no mercy, an' I'ca feel my body swellin', achin', but I couldn' stop. I couldn' 'ford to stop."*

Her gaze drifted to the ceiling for a moment, her mind traveling back to those difficult years, perhaps trying to summon the strength she'd had back then to keep pushing through.

"Da mens would work da fields wit dey machetes, an' I, I would work rhet 'longside 'em, jus slower. I couldn' 'ford tuh lose my job. I couldn' 'ford tuh stay home." She paused, her eyes meeting mine now, and I could feel the weight of her words sink in. *"You see, yo' gran'fatha had done passed on. When you out dere on yo' own, wit no help, you do what you have tuh do. Ain't nobody cared if you was pregnan. You worked, or you didn' eat."*

Her voice grew soft with the memory, and I could tell she had gone back to a place that was both painful and familiar. She was tough, but there were scars in her words.

As she spoke, a quiet tension built in my chest. I tried to imagine being in her shoes—carrying life inside me but having no choice but to keep working in harsh conditions. She did it because she had to, because there was no safety net, no cushion of support. I could feel the weight of those words pressing down on me. That's when I knew, deep down, that I would not repeat her path.

Growing up in the 1980s, I could see how things were shifting around us. I watched as families around me struggled to make ends meet. The economy was changing, and the era of single-income households was quickly fading into the past. The cost of living had been rising steadily, and the idea of providing for a family on just one income seemed increasingly unrealistic. My own parents had to work hard, and I saw the toll it took on them—emotionally, physically, and financially.

I remember watching my father come home exhausted after a long day of work. My mother, too, worked tirelessly to keep the household running smoothly. I saw how their partnership helped them weather the challenges, but I also saw the strain. I learned early on that raising a family required more than just love—it required security, stability, and a guarantee of support. Those weren't things my grandmother had, and she had to endure a lot because of it.

At the time, I was still a young girl, but I was already thinking ahead. I wasn't sure when I would start my own family, but I knew one thing: I needed to feel certain that I would have a solid foundation before making that choice. The thought of going through pregnancy alone, without the assurance of support from a partner, terrified me. I watched as single mothers struggled, and I noticed how many of them had to balance the burdens of work, childcare, and financial stress all on their own. I couldn't imagine going through something like that.

The idea of getting married before starting a family became a logical and rational decision for me. I saw it as the best way to ensure I had the support I would need—emotionally, financially, and practically. It wasn't just about love; it was about shared responsibility and partnership. The financial landscape of those times and beyond made it clear that a two-income household was not just a luxury but a necessity in many cases. The costs of raising a child—education, healthcare, housing—had become too great for one person to shoulder alone.

And so, as I grew older, I held on to that decision. I told myself that, when the time came, I would marry first. I needed to know that my partner and I would be able to support each other and our child in the best way possible. I didn't want to repeat the mistakes of the past, and I certainly didn't want to put myself in a position where I would have to make the impossible choice between work and family, as my grandmother had.

Now, as I reflect on her story, I understand the depth of her strength. She was a woman who fought to survive, who carried the weight of the world on her shoulders. But I also recognize the price she paid. Her choices, dictated by circumstance, shaped the way I would approach life. I learned from her strength, but I also learned from the limitations that came with being forced into such a difficult position. It was that balance—her unyielding will and the reality of her struggles—that taught me to approach life with a sense of caution and careful planning.

Her story shaped me in ways I never expected, and it gave me a sense of purpose that I carry with me to this day. It taught me that while strength is important, it's just as crucial to ensure that the foundation you build your life on is solid, so that the struggles you face don't have to be fought alone. My grandma was such a strong-willed woman, and here, on this night, in my weakness, I was putting her memory to shame.

CHAPTER TWO

INDEPENDENT

*"The greatest gifts we can give our children are the roots of
responsibility and the wings of independence."*
— Maria Montessori

My dad met my mom when they were barely teenagers. Their
backyards abutted, but with three acres of land, trees and bushes
betwixt and between those backyards, they didn't meet until my
dad was old enough to be sent to my grandparents' store to buy
something. My mom was working the cash register and the two
had eyes for each other.

They went to different schools but would see each other several
times over the next few years, eventually growing to become a
couple just after high school, marrying and having us three
children. Valedictorian of his class, my dad was a standout in
several ways, with one of the most literal being his 6'6" stature.
He was very tall and very slim. My mom used to say that he
weighed about 150 pounds soaking wet.

She was almost a full foot shorter, standing at 5'7". Previously a
popular majorette, mom was a beautiful woman with big brown
eyes, full cheeks, a generous smile and a larger than average

build. She wore her dark brown hair styled in a long-layered pixie cut.

A very curious child, I remember that time I got myself into trouble by trying to emulate her daily routine of carefully lining her eyes with black liner and dressing her lips with her favorite fine wine-colored lipstick. That day, I spent the morning gazing up at her as she hurriedly dressed for a funeral and ensured her face had the right look. I watched intently with a newly hatched desire to look pretty, too.

After seeing her off by standing outside in the rock covered driveway and rapidly waving my little hand at the car until she had driven out of view, I immediately and enthusiastically set off to execute the plan of action that would eventually result in a stinging ass whooping.

Once I could only see dust in the distance, I ran about 30 yards then reached out for the handrail as I hurried up the concrete steps.

The red brick house was old but sturdy, and had a deep, screened in porch. The screen door was basically a perennial fixture as it seemed to need repair or replacement at least two times each year. The grown-ups said it was because we were "bad assed kids" and kept punching through the screens. My more mature perspective tells me the screen doors were just cheap, and we were *innocent*!

Scuttling across the porch, I dash inside the house and dart through the living room. Now in the dining room, I slow down a bit and make a hard right, bursting through the curtains to enter the den. The curtains were up in a doorway. There was no door... just the curtains. Ironically, these too operated as perennial fixtures, for the same reason as the screen door. Us "bad assed kids" kept pulling them down!

These curtains were always, dependably ugly, and usually made of leftover materials from when my mom used to sew patterns for bell bottoms and other clothes.

I would enjoy sitting up until past midnight helping my mom rethread the sewing machine. So proud of her for having the skills to create clothes at home, I would gaze in admiration at the McCall's patterns, sewing needles, thread and scraps strewn about the dining room table.

Hustling past the long, white deep freezer, and old, dull yellow colored washer and dryer, I finally arrived at the small bathroom my parents had built as an add-on to supplement the household. This was a full bathroom, but had only a shower stall, rather than a shower tub combination. I took a special interest in this bathroom and always did what I could to keep it nice and clean.

Waiting exactly where I had seen her leave it was my mom's makeup case. Fairly small and easy to misplace, her black pouch had a red, pink and green rose embroidered on the outside of it. The inside was originally covered with a plastic liner, but over time that liner became dry, cracked and a nuisance. One day, mom emptied out the case and cleared out all the liner, shaking the debris into a trash can.

The make-up she maintained was modest and consisted of just an eyeliner pencil, a tube of mascara, and the dark red colored tube of lipstick. For mom, wearing makeup hadn't been ingrained into her psyche since birth. My grandma instilled in her an interest in self-improvement and well-being, which she passed down to us. So, she always took great care to make sure she was presentable before leaving the house.

I still remember, the local Avon lady was annoyingly consistent with her weekly appointments to stop by and attempt to force my grandma or mom to buy something from her catalog. My grandma, being so good-natured and kind-hearted had amassed a stockpile of roll-on deodorants, greasy lotions, stinky perfumes, body powders and sweet-smelling bubble baths that would give us bladder infections.

Though eager to share her stash of nonessential pity purchases with us, my grandma did have a favorite collection, and she often told us not to mess with her "good stuff". Even so, I can still remember that lightly spiced vanilla aroma that distinguished the *Sweet Honesty* products from the rest. As I grew older, the *Imari* roll-on deodorant became a staple in my book bag when I switched from *Tussy*, but I never lost my undying love for the smell of *Sweet Honesty*.

It had been many years in the making. On a consistent basis, I'd watched my mom apply her makeup. I studied her technique. Surely by now I was an expertly trained make-up artist!

That day, I grabbed up the eyeliner pencil with my right hand and gently pulled my lid to the side with my left hand. From my studies, I knew this was important to get a straight and complete line. With the skin tightly stretched, I used the recently sharpened pencil to slowly move the tip across my upper lid. Nothing happened. I expected to see a black trail across my skin, but there was none.

Perplexed, I quickly released my lid and moved the pencil down to see what I could see. Confirming that I had indeed removed the cap from the eyeliner pencil, I then inspected it to determine if there was a button to press or some other means of activation that I had overlooked. I didn't see anything.

Committed to this endeavor, I then attempted to draw a line on the backside of my hand. After this try also failed, I gave it another shot, this time applying a little bit of pressure. It worked!

I had figured out how to make the pencil draw but was now concerned that applying the makeup might hurt. Perhaps it wasn't intended for use by five-year-olds?

Brave and persistent, I was able to successfully line both my upper and lower eyelids with the black eyeliner. This was the toughest part as applying the mascara and lipstick were both much easier and user friendly.

I intentionally hid away from my siblings for the next couple hours. It was easy to accomplish this since they constantly ignored me anyway. From what I could understand, I was only there to be used by my older siblings to do personal errands like bringing toilet paper to the bathroom door, to ignorantly and naively go on the front lines to ask my parents the impossible requests, and to be consistently blamed for things that I *certainly* did not do.

The way I remember it, everyone was always too busy to pay attention to me, so I quickly became self-sufficient. One of my greatest personal accomplishments on record was when I finally learned to make cereal without also making a mess!

With no one noticing, I was able to maintain my flawless look until mom returned home from the funeral. When she pulled up into the driveway, I shot off the porch running straight towards the car. She was already yelling and flailing her hand as she exited the car.

"Yo lil ass done been in my makeup?! Who put that shit on your face May-May?!" My name is May Angelique Young, but everyone in my family calls me May-May.

Naively confused about her unanticipated discontent, I instantly regrouped then keenly made a futile effort to explain myself. As could've been expected, the consequences of misbehaving came swiftly. They always did.

She whooped my ass on the spot.

In my eagerness to make her proud of me, I somehow missed it when she reached out to pull it. *Fresh.* When I saw it fiercely coming at me, I suddenly regretted that I had chosen to wear short pants that morning.

I wasn't at all sorry about playing in the makeup—that was fun, and I couldn't wait to do it again! I had no concern for *when* she actually had time to remove the leaves from the thing. No, with the first sting biting into my thigh, all I could think of was how much time I wasted trying to figure out how to use that dumb eyeliner pencil. It was a slight challenge, and I really felt like giving up, but a good thing I did not because I was now earning myself some guaranteed, good sleep out there in the front yard!

As she repeatedly lit into my skin with the wet switch from our China ball tree, I wanted so badly to yell out *"the eye pencil is cheap anyway!"* but soon became disinterested in that idea.

I let out a few sincere wails, then started repeatedly saying, *"I'm sorry!!"* This was a trick I learned to convey that the mission had been accomplished. I always knew that no matter how much it did or didn't hurt, I *had to* dance around like I was stepping on hot rocks. And while it was imperative to allow at least 5-6 strikes before I cried out, it would be *ok* to start saying, *"I'm sorry"* after that sixth blow.

Children need corrections in their thinking and behavior, and my family chose the belt and the switch to implement those corrections. The idea is to remember that while they are not trying to kill you, a lesson is to be taught.

If you cry on the first sting and it's barely a tap, then you might be seen as exaggerating or even worse—you might inadvertently mess up your timing for when you're supposed to start sobbing. Then, if you're late with the crying, you run the risk of insulting the enforcer. You have to cry out and say, *"I'm sorry"*, because no child wants to hear, *"Oh you take me to play with?!"* That's a verbal assurance that the intensity of the stings will increase, as well as the duration.

It's like a rite of passage. If you were a curious kid like me, you'd learn the routine and your own personal recipe for success and then get used to it.

———

Being the youngest of the family left me ill-suited to socializing but better equipped to enjoy my own company. I always struggled with engagement but was ever creative, making the most of a fervent imagination. My resourceful attitude is what inspired my out-of-the-box thinking. I frequently got up to my own mischief and unlike that day, I was rarely found out.

Even though I was allergic to bees, I loved the outdoors. I remember planting trees, maintaining flower beds and even working gardens with tomatoes and bell peppers.

Innovative and imaginative, I explored the area by myself and often acted out some very heroic deeds! Living a full childhood, I raised families, fought dragons, dived in oceans, ran businesses, won motor races, taught classes, climbed mountains, cooked meals, flew in fighter planes, performed life-saving operations, and hid as a spy; all of which occurred within the limits of our own backyard.

My siblings couldn't care less about the outdoors. My sister was nine years my senior and my brother, six. They both always treated me as if I were a nuisance or something else, equally annoying.

I remember when I was learning how to read, and they would be so angry at me for going in their things trying to get and read all their books. Of course I was not yet suited for the advanced materials, but once I was old enough to understand what reading was, I knew I had to start doing it.

I became interested in reading mostly because I watched my dad read the newspaper every morning with a cup of coffee. He would sit there, so focused and content, then when he would speak, my mom or grandma or my siblings would all have smiling faces. Sometimes, they would laugh. Whatever the reaction, at a young age, I was able to see him looking at that thing and then saying words, producing positive emotion.

Incredibly independent for my age, from my grandma I learned the important things like how to cook eggs and rice without burning myself, and how to safely make cinnamon toast in the bottom of the oven without burning the house down.

Everything wasn't always a win, though. I also remember the time that I was home, out sick from school, and still managed to find myself in trouble.

Honestly, I was just beginning to learn the concept of multitasking, and I was absolutely innocent! In my defense, I was simply trying to maintain my appetite and save time when I stopped by the fridge to grab a slice of cheese to eat while I sat on the toilet. My dad came by the bathroom door to check on me and appeared to blow *several* gaskets seeing me sitting up there with my feet swinging and using both hands to hold on to a half-eaten slice of yellow American cheese.

"What in the hell?!", he said as his eyebrows tightened and lowered. *"I know your goddamn ass is NOT eating food in the*

bathroom, May-May?!"

Utterly shocked and completely confused, I responded,
"Yes, Sir."

My eyes had suddenly drained of the initial merriment and were beginning to prickle with tears. I wasn't used to him talking at me so hard like that. I thought he would have been proud of me for accomplishing so much during one commercial break. Did he not see how well I was balancing myself up there?! I was expecting commendations not condemnations!

———

My mom and dad were the epitome of hard work and dedication, yet despite their relentless efforts, we often found ourselves struggling to make ends meet. My mother, Linda, worked as a secretary at a predominantly Caucasian-owned business. She was the backbone of the office, the one who kept everything running smoothly, yet her paycheck never seemed to reflect her true value. It was a frustrating reality that she faced every day, knowing that her skills and dedication were not being fairly compensated. Despite this, she carried herself with grace and dignity, always putting her best foot forward.

My father, August Sr., was equally industrious. He worked as a maintenance supervisor at a factory 60 miles away—a job that demanded long hours and physical labor. He took pride in his work, ensuring that everything was in top shape, but like my mother, his efforts were not rewarded with a salary that matched his dedication. The factory was a place where he poured his sweat and energy, yet the financial returns were modest at best.

Even with both of them working tirelessly, there were times when it felt like one step forward was followed by two steps back. Unexpected expenses would crop up, and the little savings they managed to put aside would quickly dwindle. It was a constant balancing act, trying to stretch every dollar to cover the essentials while also providing for me and my siblings.

Despite these challenges, my parents were incredibly charitable. They believed in helping others whenever they could, often giving away what little they had to those in need. It was not uncommon for them to invite a struggling neighbor over for dinner or to donate clothes to a family who had fallen on hard times. Their generosity was a testament to their character, teaching me the importance of compassion and community.

Because my parents worked so much, I spent a lot of time with my grandmother. She was my rock, the one who provided stability and comfort when my parents were busy trying to keep our family afloat. Her home, then just a few dozen yards away from ours, was a sanctuary, a place where I could escape the worries of the world and find solace in her stories and wisdom.

Growing up in this environment taught me resilience and the value of hard work. It also instilled in me a deep appreciation for the sacrifices my parents made and the love they showed, not just to our family, but to everyone around them. Their example was a guiding light, showing me that even in the face of adversity, kindness and generosity could prevail.

Around the age of six, I found myself stepping into a new realm of independence. With my older siblings already out the door, embarking on their own daily adventures, and my parents having left early for work, the responsibility of getting ready for school fell squarely on my small shoulders. Each morning, I would shuffle through my modest wardrobe, piecing together outfits that I hoped would pass muster in the schoolyard. It was a solitary ritual, one that I performed quietly in the early hours, the house still and silent around me.

My grandmother, who was in her sixties and battling the relentless grip of arthritis, was my only company during these mornings. Her presence was a comforting constant, even if her physical ability to assist was limited. She would sit in her favorite chair, offering gentle encouragement and the occasional piece of advice as I navigated the complexities of buttons and zippers. Her wisdom was a guiding light, even if her hands could no longer help with the practical tasks.

By the time I turned seven, I had grown weary of the three-day-old fuzzy hair look. Despite my mother's efforts, my hair seemed to have a mind of its own. When my next-door neighbor kindly offered to do my hair, I eagerly went over one morning, excited to let her style it for me. At first, everything felt fine—her help was warm and welcoming. But that changed when her daughter went to school and told everyone that I had to go to their house because my mom didn't know how to do my hair. That moment stung deeper than I could put into words. It wasn't just about the teasing—it was the realization that seeking help could leave me vulnerable to ridicule. From that day on, a quiet but powerful belief began to take root in me: *Never ask for help*. It was a lesson learned in a painful way, and one that would stay with me for much longer than I ever expected.

Determined to take control of my appearance, I began the arduous process of learning to style my own hair. It was a challenge, to say the least, but one that I approached with the same determination that had seen me through countless mornings of dressing myself. I would stand in front of the mirror, comb in hand, experimenting with different styles until I found something that felt right. It was a small victory, but a significant one, marking the beginning of a journey towards self-reliance that would shape much of my childhood.

All said, I often felt like a ghost in my own home, my presence acknowledged but rarely celebrated. My parents and siblings, though inherently kind and patient, were often consumed by their own important lives, leaving little room for open displays of affection. Their constant busyness, while unintentional, made me feel like an afterthought, a quiet observer in the background of their achievements. Despite their good intentions, the lack of explicit warmth and attention left me feeling like a burden, a sentiment I carried silently.

It didn't resonate until I was older, but it was such a blessing that we lived so close to our grandma because I really capitalized on the relationship that I had with her. She was just like a best friend and taught me so much. There are so many things that she has said to me about life, but I didn't understand until years later.

"Life is not always easy tuh live, but da opportunity tuh do so is a blessin' beyon comprehension."

I hear the words echoing in my mind. I feel an overpowering sense of guilt because the way I feel right now is...beyond comprehension.

CHAPTER THREE

STUDIOUS

*"What lies behind us and what lies before us are tiny matters
compared to what lies within us."*
— *Ralph Waldo Emerson*

I've always been the quiet one, the observer in the corner,
soaking in the world around me. I suppose you could say I'm a
bit of an enigma, even to myself.

Growing up as the youngest of three, I often felt like I was living
in the shadows of my older siblings. They were always so
vibrant, so sure of themselves, while I was the lanky, introverted
one, more comfortable with my nose in a book than in the midst
of a crowd.

School was my sanctuary. I thrived in the structured
environment, where my intelligence and creativity could flourish
without the pressure of social expectations. Stellar marks came
naturally to me, but with them came the weight of others'
expectations.

People saw my academic success and assumed I had everything
figured out, but inside, I was just a girl trying to understand her

place in the world.

I remember my school years as a time of both challenge and triumph, where I discovered my potential and began to carve out my identity through a series of academic and personal achievements. These experiences not only shaped my character but also laid the foundation for my future endeavors. Let me take you on a journey through some of the most memorable accomplishments from those formative years.

In the eighties, I was in elementary school, a time when most children were just beginning to explore their interests and talents. For me, it was a period of discovery and dedication. I was awarded the top prize at my school, known as *The Good Egg Award*. This accolade was not just a testament to my academic prowess but also a symbol of my commitment and perseverance. The award itself was unique—a real ostrich egg, meticulously hollowed out and cleaned, then mounted on a wooden plaque. It was a tangible reminder of my hard work and the recognition I received for maintaining straight A's throughout my elementary school career. But it wasn't just about the grades. I also had perfect attendance, which spoke to my dedication and reliability. Beyond academics, I was actively involved in volunteer activities, always eager to lend a helping hand and be a dependable friend to my peers. This award was a celebration of my holistic approach to school life, where kindness and diligence went hand in hand.

Fast forward, and I found myself in middle school, a time of transition and new challenges. It was during this period that I discovered my passion for writing. I participated in an impromptu writing competition, an event that required us to enter a room with nothing but a pencil and a piece of notebook paper. We were given a topic and a set amount of time to craft our response.

The pressure was intense, but I thrived under it. I was the only student from my entire middle school to place in the entire convention, securing second place as a sixth grader! This achievement was significant not only because of the recognition it brought but also because it affirmed my talent as a writer. Representing my school in such a prestigious event was an honor, and it fueled my desire to continue honing my writing skills.

By grade eight, I had developed a deep love for languages, particularly French. This passion led me to enter an international writing contest, open to middle and high school students worldwide. The challenge was to write an essay entirely in French, describing someone or something important to us. I chose to write about my relationship with my grandmother who had always been a source of inspiration and love in my life. Crafting the essay was a labor of love, and I poured my heart into every word. To my astonishment and delight, I won first place in the contest! The prize was a French-manufactured camera, and the contest sponsor featured my full essay in the Spring publication of a French magazine! This achievement brought me into the spotlight—I was featured in the local newspaper, interviewed on the local news, and invited to several speaking engagements. At just 12 years old, I was experiencing the thrill of international recognition, and it was a moment I would cherish forever.

These accomplishments during my early school years were more than just accolades; they were milestones that marked my journey of self-discovery and growth. Each success taught me valuable lessons about perseverance, passion, and the power of words. They were the building blocks of my future, instilling in me the confidence to pursue my dreams and the resilience to overcome any obstacles that came my way. Looking back, I am grateful for these experiences and the opportunities they provided to learn, grow, and shine.

Despite my achievements, I struggled with self-esteem. I was often told I was beautiful, but I couldn't see it. I felt like an unfinished puzzle, with pieces that didn't quite fit. My curiosity and innovative spirit were my guiding lights, leading me to explore new ideas and possibilities, but they also set me apart, making me feel like an outsider.

Honestly, I always felt like I was living in the shadows of my older siblings, June and August. They seemed to have been born with a roadmap to success, while I was still trying to figure out which direction to take. Our household was always bustling with activity, and they were the trailblazers, setting up a high bar that I often felt I couldn't reach.

June, the eldest, seemed to view me as a pawn, but simultaneously, she was a beacon of compassion and patience. Her path to becoming a special education teacher was paved with a genuine love for helping others, a beautiful trait attributed to Momo. She had this incredible ability to notice the small things, the subtle shifts in mood, the unspoken words. Her empathy was her superpower, allowing her to connect with her students on a level that few could. Watching her with her students was like witnessing magic; she had a way of making each child feel seen and heard. Her marriage to David, a dentist with his own thriving practice, was a testament to her nurturing nature. Together, they were a powerful couple, balancing their demanding careers with a warm and loving home life. I admired June's ability to juggle her responsibilities with such grace, even if I never quite knew how to express it.

August, on the other hand, was the quintessential problem solver. As a mechanical engineer, his world was one of precision and logic. He had a knack for seeing the world in terms of systems and structures, always looking for ways to improve and innovate. His marriage to Emily, a fellow engineer, was a partnership built on mutual respect and shared ambitions. They had two children, who were as inquisitive and bright as their parents. August's life seemed to be a well-oiled machine, running smoothly and efficiently, much like the projects he worked on. His confidence was palpable, a stark contrast to the self-doubt that often plagued me.

Despite their differences, June and August shared a close bond, one that was rooted in a deep understanding of each other's strengths and weaknesses. They were supportive of each other, celebrating successes and offering comfort during setbacks. This camaraderie, however, sometimes left me feeling like an extra, as if I were watching a play from the wings, never quite stepping into the spotlight.

My perception of myself as the "failure" of the family was a narrative I had constructed over the years. It wasn't that June and August ever explicitly labeled me as such; rather, it was the silent comparison, the unspoken expectations that weighed heavily on my shoulders. I longed for their approval, for a nod of recognition that I was on the right path, even if it was different from theirs.

June and August, in their own ways, were aware of my struggles. June, with her keen sense of empathy, often sensed the undercurrents of insecurity in me. She tried to reach out, to offer words of encouragement, but her efforts sometimes fell short, lost in translation. August, ever the pragmatist, believed in leading by example. He hoped that by showing me the value of hard work and perseverance, I would find my own way to success.

Yet, in their attempts to support me, they inadvertently reinforced the very pressures I felt. Their successes, while inspiring, were also intimidating. My decision to leave town for college was, in part, an attempt to carve out my own identity, away from the looming shadows of my siblings. It was supposed to be my escape, my chance to reinvent myself. I was eager to step out of my comfort zone, to embrace the unknown. But life has a way of throwing curveballs. After graduation, I returned home, jobless and uncertain. The weight of my perceived failures felt even heavier.

Navigating the professional world was a journey I never anticipated would be so fraught with challenges and lessons. A full three years out of college, with a failed business under my belt, I was eager to prove myself, but the reality of my first big girl job was a harsh awakening. My supervisor, an older, married church deacon, seemed to take an inappropriate interest in me. At first, I brushed off his comments, thinking I was misinterpreting his intentions. But as his advances became more overt and obnoxious, I knew I had to stand my ground. When I finally told him to stop, his demeanor shifted dramatically. Suddenly, I was assigned the toughest projects, and he frequently threatened me with termination, knowing I was still on probation. The fear of losing my first job after eleven months of unemployment left me paralyzed. I felt trapped, unable to speak out, and my mental health began to suffer under the weight of his retaliation.

In my next role, I encountered a unique challenge. My supervisor, a younger Indian woman, seemed threatened by my experience and merit. It felt as though my intelligence and success were perceived as a direct threat to her own standing. This perception might have been influenced by her upbringing and familial social stigmas, where societal expectations often place immense pressure on individuals to succeed and maintain a certain image. She acted as if my achievements highlighted her own perceived shortcomings, leading her to undermine me by misinforming leadership about my work and painting me in a negative light. Despite my solid efforts and dedication, I missed out on a promotion because of her jealousy. She was known for her bullying tactics, with several EEO complaints against her, but I never filed one myself. I held onto my faith, believing that 'vengeance is Mine,' as God said. Yet, the constant stress took a toll on my mental health.

On the surface, once you scraped off the calculated and conniving behavior of my immature supervisor, I appeared to be thriving—receiving commendations, taking on more responsibilities, and maintaining a facade of self-regulation and reliability. However, beneath that exterior, I was struggling with a profound sense of despair. My days were a blur of obligations, and my nights were spent in a haze of exhaustion. I would retreat to my bed as soon as I got home, using sleep as an escape from the overwhelming heaviness that seemed to cling to me.

I didn't recognize it as depression at the time. I just felt perpetually tired, both physically and emotionally. It was as if I was carrying an invisible weight that made every task feel monumental. Despite my achievements at work, I felt like a failure, unable to shake the feeling that I was merely going through the motions of life without truly living it.

My coworkers and friends remained oblivious to my internal struggle. I had become adept at masking my pain, smiling through the day and offering help to others, all while feeling isolated and misunderstood. It was a lonely existence, where the fear of being exposed as vulnerable kept me from reaching out for help. I was trapped in a cycle of high performance and deepening depression, unsure of how to break free.

I was raised to be accountable and hardworking, but I struggled to balance my career ambitions with the toxic environments I found myself in.

The final straw came in a *second role* where I had various leadership assignments but was repeatedly passed over for promotions that went to less qualified Caucasian coworkers. I was the reliable one, the teammate who never dropped the ball, always anticipating problems and managing crises. But I learned the hard way that reliability is not job security; it's a trauma response. My competence meant I was burdened with the most complex projects and other people's emotional labor, leaving my own tasks sometimes undone. I finally realized that my worth wasn't measured by the disasters I prevented or the emergencies I managed. I had to learn to let go, to understand that "I trust you to figure this out" is a complete sentence. Dropping balls strategically became a necessary skill.

I remember the day it all started to unravel. I was sitting at my desk, staring at the endless stream of emails flooding my inbox, each one demanding my immediate attention. My heart raced, and my stomach churned—a familiar feeling that had become my constant companion. I was known for my exceptional work ethic, my ability to juggle multiple projects with ease, and my unwavering commitment to perfection. But lately, I felt like I was drowning.

I had always been the go-to person in the office, the friendliest one who could also be relied upon to take on extra tasks and deliver results that exceeded expectations. My leadership seemed to have no qualms about piling more work onto my plate, confident that I would handle it all without complaint. And for a long time, I did. I thrived on the challenge but only because I saw it as a way to prove myself. The actual recognition came in dribbles while the sense of accomplishment came in droves ...initially. I had personal goals to reach a certain point in my career, and by the time I came to this team, I was two years behind schedule due to the due to the unethical shenanigans of that Indian supervisor. I gave it my best, but somewhere along the way, I lost sight of myself.

The signs of burnout were there, but I was uneducated about them. I was irritable, nearly snapping at colleagues over minor issues. I was becoming increasingly more like a zombie. My concentration was shot, and I found myself rereading the same paragraph multiple times without absorbing a word. Even outside of the office, I was forgetful, missing personal deadlines and appointments that I would never have overlooked before. I even struggled to get to group meetups. And the physical symptoms—headaches, stomachaches, and a constant feeling of exhaustion—were impossible to ignore.

It was during one particularly grueling week that I had an epiphany. I was working late, as usual, when I realized that my definition of *"half-assing"* my work was equivalent to others' *"whole-assing* theirs."* Throughout my career, I had been giving 120% of myself to my job, but what if I could give less—say, 60%—and still be more than competent? The thought was both terrifying and liberating.

I decided to experiment. I stopped responding to emails the moment they arrived, allowing myself to prioritize and tackle them in batches. I no longer sought "learning opportunities" by volunteering for projects outside of my immediate responsibilities, focusing instead on doing my core tasks well. I took regular breaks, stepping away from my desk to clear my mind and recharge. And most importantly, I stopped working past my shift. When the workday ended, I shut down my computer and left the office, leaving work behind.

At first, I felt guilty. I worried that I would let my team down, that my performance would suffer, that I would be seen as lazy or uncommitted. But to my surprise, none of that happened. While I was still never promoted, my work remained of high quality, and I was still being sought after by other divisions.

As I adjusted to this new way of working, I began to feel a slight sense of relief. The damage of burnout was definitely still there, however the constant pressure I had been placing on myself started to lift, and I found that I had a little more energy and patience, both at work and in my personal life. I was no longer defined solely by my job; I was very slowly rediscovering who I was outside of the office.

This awakening was the first lesson of many, in understanding the importance of setting boundaries and prioritizing my well-being. I learned that it was okay to say no, to delegate tasks, and to ask for help when needed. I realized that my worth was not determined by how much I could accomplish in a day, but by the quality of my soul and the balance I maintained in my life.

Through these experiences, I matured. It took years and countless small lessons, but I finally understood that my mental health was paramount. I decided that in my next role, I would let others own their work, stop anticipating problems that weren't mine, and protect my mental bandwidth—at all costs. Carrying the whole team wasn't dedication; it was exhaustion in disguise. This realization marked the beginning of my journey to reclaim my mental health, a long and arduous path, but one I was finally ready to embark on.

CHAPTER FOUR

FRUITLESS

"In everyone's life, at some time, our inner fire goes out. It is then burst into flame by an encounter with another human being. We should all be thankful for those people who rekindle the inner spirit."
— Albert Schweitzer

"It is so fancy in here, I hope they don't embarrass me," I thought. Needing to reset my mind, I executed my go-to breathing exercise. "Two, three, four...". My feet planted firmly on the floor, I realize I am not focusing enough. I start to feel anxious but quickly switch my thoughts.

"What's happening with you?", I ask myself.

"I'm getting nervous.", I responded in my head.

"Bitch why?! There's nothing to be pre-worrying about, you're just sitting in a lobby! We're not doing this today! Cut it out!"

Slowly exhaling through my mouth, I can feel the tension releasing from my soul. As I unclench my fists and open my eyes, I hear my grandma tell me *"rejection is God's protection.*

An opportunity fuh redirection".

"Thank you, grandma.", I say to myself.

Calmer, I am now able to enjoy the elegant and upscale interior of this place. I'd become familiar with the typical look and feel of my local community bank, so the high ceilings and wide marble columns with fluted edges were very impressive! The floors were made of large, super shiny white looking tiles. I'm sure the official color must've been opal or Mother of Pearl of something fancy, but in this description, just picture a glossy white, wet looking floor.

I'd never seen anything like this in person. There were massive windows that ran floor to ceiling and wide complementary designer rugs. Similar to a grand hotel lobby, there were spacious sitting areas with leather couches, oversized swivel chairs, and heavy coffee tables. I'm sure the design was to accommodate larger groups who probably flew into town on a private jet.

Enthralled, I was just noticing the various paintings, artwork, and marble sculptures when a tall black man entered my line of sight.

He was handsome.

The closer he got to me, the more I fell in love. Instinctively, I trained my eyes on his hands. They were impossibly enormous, but curiously young looking. Remembering my initial curiosity, I noticed that there are no rings on these flawlessly manicured gigantic man hands. So naturally, I transitioned to *"In Love: Phase II".*

This is the phase where I commit wholeheartedly to unavailable partners while denying their incompatibility. Over the years, I became really proficient at romanticizing men, with little to no evidence that they are worth a damn. As dumb as it sounds, I made a habit of committing to partners before getting to know their values and learning about them. I usually follow up with feeling completely crushed when the reality of who they actually are sets in.

Once I learn about their unavailability, I instinctively choose to be dishonest with myself for as long as I can manage. I would keep holding on to nonexistent hope, refusing to move on from the romantic delusion, which sometimes would take years. So now, at 32 years old, having not yet learned when a man pursues a woman, it is often seen as a demonstration of confidence and initiative, I was ready shoot my shot and risk it all!

He was handsome. From the depth of his eyes to the gentle expression of his voice.

"Ms. Young?". He sounded like *my husband.*

"Yes, babe?", I thought as I stood up with my right hand outreached.

"Good morning!", I said with a wide grin as his hand swallowed mine.

So much power, his over-enthusiastic handshake would have definitely snapped my wrist in two if I had weak bones.

"I'm Julian Ingram, the head of Small Business Banking here at CG Bank."

He. Was. Handsome. From his generous scent to the touch of his hand upon my own. I was now in *"Phase III"*...and I think I'm pregnant!

He led me to his office. Enclosed by floor to ceiling glass walls, as we arrived, I could see there was a dark walnut bookcase lining the entire right-hand wall. There was a leather sofa that matched the ones in the lobby with a fur rug over the back and a fluffy blanket draped over the arm. The far wall had a large television dominating the center, with two floating mantles lining it on either side. On the mantles, were two antique clocks and two different paintings of jazz musicians. In the far corner was an upright piano and bench in dark walnut. A piano! Hanging on the wall above the piano was an abstract painting of three jazz musicians. There was a double door between his desk and the piano, which leads out to the limestone paved patio. The patio!

Even from here I could see some breathtaking city views!

Although I'm wearing a pleasant facial expression, I'm not really present. I haven't heard a word he's said. To the left behind me is a bookshelf atop a file cabinet. The ceiling fan keeps the soft air moving throughout the open space.

Curiously, there were no family photos displayed in the entire office.

"I'm loving the style of this space, and yes, I'll marry you, but what about family? Do you want us to have a family?".
Suddenly, I'm back. I'm present. I tune back in just in time for the closing:

*"To be frank, with my 16 years in the banking industry, it's obvious that business owners like yourself need to understand how much money is flowing through their operations. If more money is going out than coming in, then you need to make changes. As a standard practice, if your business has too tight of a margin, you should work toward lowering expenses or finding ways to grow revenue **before** applying for a loan,"* said Mr. Ingram.

He was handsome alright, but inside he was a fucking asshole effortlessly ruining my life. The wedding was off!

With his words, I'd just died a private death. I needed this loan to be approved. Managing the huge disappointment, somehow, I was able to remain professional and respectful as he escorted me out to the lobby. I quickly noticed that it wasn't all that fancy anymore. Just gaudy and excessive, if I'm being honest.

Sitting in my car, I find myself in tears. How can this be? They said the third time is the charm, but this was my fourth denial. In pieces, I begin to mentally process the situation. But as a prelude, I think of my teachings and remind myself of myself:

"I am happy with my progress and my growth. Obstacles do not deter me; they only push me to go for more. I am tuned in and aligned with who I am, and I trust my ability to pursue my success."

"Damnit!" I say out loud as the call to my grandma goes to voicemail. I'm in need of some immediate reassurance and strength, so I head towards route 19. To grandma's house we go.

As I pull up the driveway I can see her out there in the garden. She's by the tomatoes.

This house was anchored in love. There were always so many plants and flowers everywhere. Still pulling tomatoes from the vine, she doesn't see me approaching her.

Then, she stops and gets up.

So impressive. Even in my shattered state, I could acknowledge that my Momo still had it! She continued to look spry. Just like when I was growing up, she still walked two miles into town and back each Saturday and she was now well into her eighties.

"What's wrong baby? Yo' makeup. You been cryin'?", she asked, blurting out the words in an urgent concerned tone.

Diverting my eyes from hers, I focused on her earring—a small golden heart that complemented her amazing skin. Within reach, I effortlessly outstretched my arms to accept the warm embrace. I was safe in her arms with my head cradled on her shoulder before all the colors blurred and blended together. Soon, I could feel the warm tickle of fresh tears rolling down my face. I couldn't prevent the shudder that rocked through me when she said, *"I'm here, baby—it's all goin' tuh be ok."*

I believed her.

Still unable to compose myself, I hadn't yet uttered a word. She continued to squeeze me, and the calming words never ceased. After a few moments, she loosened the embrace and suggested that we go to sit down on the back porch.

———————

As I step up onto the back porch, the familiar creak of the wooden boards beneath my feet brings a comforting sense of nostalgia. The backyard stretches out before me, a vibrant tapestry of life and color that has been lovingly tended to over the years. This space, with its gentle hum of activity, feels like an extension of myself—a place where memories are woven into the very fabric of the earth.

The vegetable garden is the heart of this backyard, a testament to the seasons and the passage of time. Neat rows of tomatoes, their vines heavy with ripe, red fruit, stand proudly alongside leafy greens that sway gently in the breeze. The earthy scent of soil mingles with the sweet aroma of basil and mint, creating a symphony of fragrances that envelops me in a warm embrace. I can almost taste the freshness of the produce, recalling the countless summer evenings spent picking vegetables for dinner, my hands stained with the rich, dark soil.

Beyond the vegetable garden lies the flower garden, a riot of colors that dances in the sunlight. Delicate petals of every hue— vibrant yellows, deep purples, and soft pinks—create a living mosaic that shifts and changes with the light. The flowers nod their heads in the gentle wind, as if acknowledging my presence. Bees buzz industriously from bloom to bloom, their tiny bodies dusted with pollen, while butterflies flit gracefully through the air, adding a touch of whimsy to the scene.

In the corner of the yard, the clothesline stands as a sentinel of domesticity, its lines strung with freshly laundered sheets and clothes that billow like sails in the wind. The rhythmic flapping of fabric is a soothing sound, a reminder of the simple, everyday rituals that define home. I remember helping my grandmother hang the laundry here, the two of us working side by side, our laughter mingling with the rustle of the leaves overhead.

This backyard is more than just a garden; it is a sanctuary, a place where the world slows down and the soul finds peace. It is here that I spent countless hours as a child, my imagination running wild as I played games of make-believe. I can still see the outlines of the pirate ship I once commanded, the grassy expanse that served as my ocean. I remember the thrill of adventure as I battled imaginary foes, my heart racing with the excitement of discovery.

In the quiet moments, I would lie on the soft grass, staring up at the sky as clouds drifted lazily by. I would daydream of the future, imagining the person I would become and the adventures

that awaited me beyond the confines of this backyard. Those
dreams were woven into the very essence of this place, each
blade of grass a reminder of the hopes and aspirations that took
root here.

As I stand here now, I am filled with a profound sense of calm
and belonging. This backyard, with its vibrant gardens and gentle
rhythms, is a reflection of the life that has unfolded within its
embrace. It is a place where the past and present coexist, where
memories are cherished, and new ones are made. In this space, I
am home, surrounded by the beauty of nature and the echoes of a
childhood spent dreaming beneath the open sky.

———————

Grandma touches a warm wet towel to my forehead jilting me
back to reality. She asks, *"you ok? Talk tuh me baby..."*

"I'm a failure. I'm not a business lady."

"What you mean baby? Da bank ain't 'prove da loan?"

"No ma'am, they didn't."

*"Oh, my dear, come set wit me fo' a moment. I can see da worry
etched on yo' face, an' I want you tuh know dat dis setback do
not define you. Life has a way of throwin' us curveballs, an' while
it may feel like da end of da world right now, I promise you, it's
not. You uh not a failure, not by no stretch of da 'magination.*

*Rememba, every great success story has its share of obstacles.
Think of it as a steppin' stone, not a stumblin' block. You have
always been so determine an' full of dreams, an' I have no doubt
you'll find a way tuh make dis work. Da bank may have said no
ds time, but dat don't mean it's a no fo 'ever. Dere is other paths
to explore, other doars to knock on, an' I believe wit all my heart*

that you will fine da' right one.

You have a spirit dat is unyieldin' an' a mine dat is sharp an' creative. Dem qualities will serve you well as you navigate dis challenge. Take a deep breath an' allow yo'self tuh feel da disappointment, but don't let it linga too long. Instead, use it as fuel tuh propel you forward. You have da strength tuh turn dis here aroun', an' I am here tuh support you every step of da way.

Think back tuh all da times you've overcome difficulty befoe. Rememba when you won dat international writin' contest? You were just a child, yet you stood out among so many. That same resilience an' talent is within you now. You've always had a knack for findin' solutions, an' I know you'll do it again.

Let's brainstorm togetha, shall we? Dere might be otha financial institutions, grants, or even investors who would be thrilled to support someone as passionate an' driven as you. An' rememba, it's okay to ax fo' help. You have a community aroun' you dat believes in you an' wanna see you succeed.

Most importantly, don't lose sight of yo' vision. Hol' onto it tightly, nurture it, an' let it guide you. Yo' dreams is wurth fighting fo, an' I have every confidence dat you will achieve 'em. You is not alone in dis, my dear. I am here, an' I will always be here, cheerin' you on an' remindin' you of yo' wurth.

So, dry dose tears an' lift yo' chin. Dis is jus' one chap'ta in yo' story, an' I know da pages dat follow will be fill wit triump' an' joy. You is capable, you is strong, an' you is loved. Now, let's get to work on findin' a new path forward. Together, we'll make sure yo' dreams come to life."

Inside, I'm sitting at the kitchen table as grandma pours some tea for us. I couldn't believe how heavy the day had felt, nor did I know I had that much cry backed up in me. Once I started, I had been unable to stop as each and every memory of my previous failures played on a reel in my head.

I was so thankful to have Momo. She didn't force me to talk to her, she just knew that I was in pain and allowed me to feel without judgment. She consistently wiped my face with a warm, wet cloth as she reassured me that I was O.K.

With deep appreciation for the support, I became frustrated with myself because I couldn't stop the mental video from playing. I'd been trying so hard to get this right, to be successful, yet more than 10 years later, here I was sitting in my grandmother's kitchen crying…again.

"Again?! Yes, again!", I heard.

"Interiordecorating?! Girl what were you thinking?!"

"Customized gift baskets was so dumb."

"You just love to be stupid. Why did you ever think you could start your own hair care line when your own hair does nothing but look dry and break?!"

The negative thoughts were flooding in, and I couldn't stop them.

As I sat at the kitchen table, the familiar aroma of freshly brewed tea wafting through the air, I poured my heart out to Grandma. *"I've been at this for over ten years, Grandma. All these years of trying to get it right, and I'm ready to give up,"* I confessed, my voice tinged with frustration and defeat.

Momo listened intently, her eyes filled with understanding and warmth. *"Tell me bout it, dear,"* she encouraged gently, herhands wrapped around her own steaming cup.

I took a deep breath and began to recount my journey. *"The first business was supposed to be a game-changer. Interior decorating, with a twist. I thought I could save businesses and families time and energy by decorating their spaces for the holidays. Christmas, Halloween, Easter—you name it. I even offered to store and maintain all the decorations. But the costs were overwhelming, and I just couldn't keep up. I managed to serve nine businesses and four families before I had to call it quits."*

Grandma nodded; her expression thoughtful. *"That was a big undertakin', my dear. You was thinkin' ahead, tryna make life easier fo' othas."*

"Then came the custom gift basket business," I continued. *"I was so excited about creating unique gift baskets, cookie bouquets, and fruit arrangements. I even delivered them with balloons as a surprise. It started off well, but I couldn't scale up. I didn't have the experience or resources to meet the growing demand."*

"You brought joy to so many people wit dose gifts," Grandma interjected, her voice filled with pride. *"I remembas how delighted everyone was tuh receive 'em."*

And then there was the custom cake decorating business," I said, my voice softening as I recalled the sweet memories. *"I poured my heart into those cakes. People loved the designs and the flavors. I was quickly becoming the go-to cake maker in the city. But then I signed a lease for a storefront, and a so-called 'friend' of a professional colleague that I had known for nearly 10 years conned me out of $19,000. It was everything I had, Momo."* Tears began to well up in my eyes.

Grandma reached across the table and took my hand, her touch comforting and reassuring. *"You was doin' everything in yo' power tuh succeed, my dear. But sometimes, despite our bess efforts, things don't go as plan. It doesn't mean you failed. It just means dat perhaps da time or da idea at that time wasn't right."*

I looked into her eyes, searching for answers. *"But what if I'm just not meant to succeed, Momo? What if I'm not cut out for this?"*

Grandma shook her head, her gaze unwavering. *"Havin' da courage tuh try is somethin' a lot of people neva have. You dared tuh dream, tuh take risks, an' tuh put yo'sef out dere. Dat takes immense strength an' bravery. You learned an' grew wit each experience, an' dat's somethin' tuh be proud'uh."*

Her words wrapped around me like a warm embrace, soothing the ache in my heart. *"But what do I do now?"* I asked, my voice barely above a whisper.

"You keep goin', my dear," Grandma replied, her voice steady and full of conviction. *"You take what you've learn an' use it tuh build somethin' new. Rememba, every setback is a setup fo' a comeback. Trust in yo'sef an' in da journey. An' know dat I'm always here fo' you, cheerin' you on every step uh'da way."*

As I sat there, holding Momo's hand, I felt a flicker of hope reignite within me. Maybe the path to success wasn't a straight line, but a winding road filled with lessons and growth. And maybe, just maybe, I was exactly where I needed to be.

As the sun began to dip below the horizon, casting a warm, golden glow over the kitchen, Momo rose from her chair with a gentle smile. *"How 'bout we get ourselfs some ice cream, hmm? I think a little sweetness might do us both some good,"* she suggested, her voice as soothing as a lullaby. I nodded, grateful for the distraction and the comfort of her presence.

As she scooped the ice cream into bowls, Grandma began to speak, her words weaving a tapestry of encouragement and love. *"You know, my dear, I've watch you grow an' blossom into da remarkable woman you is tuh'day. Yo' resilience has always been one uh yo' greatest strengths.*

Rememba when you decided tuh start yo own hair care line? You was so innovative, always thinkin' ahead uh'da curve. It's no surprise dat independent hair care brands have become so popula now. You was jus ahead uh yo' time."

She handed me a bowl of ice cream, her eyes twinkling with pride. *"Yo mine an' creativity are truly somethin' special. You always blazin' new trails, an' while dat can make things challengin', it also make you incredibly valuable tuh society. People love yo' work, an' dat alone is a testamen' tuh yo' talent an' vision."*

I took a bite of the ice cream, letting the cool sweetness melt away some of the day's worries. Momo's words were like a balm to my soul, reminding me of the strength and creativity that had always been a part of me.

As the evening wore on, the comforting rhythm of our conversation and the familiar surroundings of Grandma's house began to wrap around me like a warm blanket. I realized that I didn't want to leave this cocoon of love and understanding just yet.

"Momo," I said softly, *"I think I might just stay the night, if that's okay with you. I took off work for a few days. I don't have anything else planned, and being here with you is exactly what I need right now."*

Grandma's face lit up with a smile that could rival the sun. *"Of course, my dear. You is always welcome here. Dere's nothin' moe importan' den feelin' seen, heard, an' loved. You ca' stay as long as you like. You know dat, baby."*

With that, we settled into the cozy comfort of the evening, the weight of the world lifting just a little as I found solace in the warmth of Momo's love and the promise of a new day.

———————

After a long, soothing bath, I wrapped myself in a plush towel, feeling the warmth seep into my bones. The steam from the bath still lingered in the air, curling around me like a comforting embrace. I took a deep breath, letting the scent of lavender and chamomile calm my racing thoughts. As I settled into bed, I whispered a quiet prayer, asking for strength and guidance. The weight of the day began to lift, and I felt a sense of peace washing over me.

Sleep came quickly, but it was not the restful slumber I had hoped for. Instead, I found myself in a dream that mirrored my deepest fears. I was standing in the middle of a bustling city street, surrounded by the remnants of my failed businesses. The decorations from my first venture lay scattered on the ground, tangled in a mess of tinsel and broken ornaments. The gift baskets from my second attempt were overturned, their contents spilling out onto the pavement. And there, in the center of it all, was the storefront I had dreamed of for my cake business, its windows dark and empty.

Around me, familiar faces appeared—friends I had known for years. But instead of offering support, they pointed and laughed, their voices echoing in my mind. *"She's a failure,"* they taunted, their words cutting deeper than any blade. I tried to defend myself, to explain that I had done everything I could, but my voice was lost in the cacophony of their laughter. I felt a crushing sense of loneliness, as if the world had turned its back on me.

Suddenly, the scene shifted, and I was standing in a field of wildflowers, the sun warm on my face. The laughter faded, replaced by the gentle rustle of the wind through the grass. I felt a presence beside me, a comforting hand on my shoulder. Though I couldn't see who it was, I felt a deep sense of love and reassurance. *"You are not alone,"* a voice whispered, and I felt a flicker of hope ignite within me.

I awoke to the smell of waffles wafting through the air, the sweet aroma pulling me from the remnants of my dream. I sat up, the morning light filtering through the curtains, casting a soft glow across the room. The dream lingered in my mind, but the warmth of the sun and the promise of a new day began to chase away the shadows.

I made my way to the kitchen, where Grandma was bustling about, her back to me as she flipped waffles on the griddle. The sight of her, so steady and sure, filled me with a sense of comfort. *"Good mornin', sweetheart,"* she said, turning to greet me with a smile. *"I made yo' favorite."*

"Thank you, Momo," I replied, taking a seat at the table. The waffles were golden and crisp, topped with fresh berries and a drizzle of syrup. As I took my first bite, the familiar flavors wrapped around me like a warm hug, and I felt a sense of gratitude for this moment, for this place that felt like home.

We ate in companionable silence, the clink of cutlery and the hum of the morning radio filling the space between us. As I finished my meal, I looked up at Momo, her eyes filled with understanding and love.

"I'm meeting with some friends later this week," I told her, a hint of uncertainty in my voice.

"Dat's wonda'fa, dear," she replied, her smile encouraging. *"Rememba, true friends will always support you, no matter what."*

Her words resonated with me, and I felt a renewed sense of determination. The dream had been unsettling, but it had also reminded me of the strength I carried within me, the resilience that had brought me this far. I knew that the road ahead would not be easy, but with Momo by my side and the promise of new beginnings, I felt ready to face whatever challenges lay ahead.

CHAPTER FIVE

STIFLED

"When someone shows you who they are, believe them the first time."
— *Maya Angelou*

As I entered the upscale lounge, the soft hum of jazz music and the gentle clinking of glasses created an ambiance of sophistication and warmth. The dim lighting cast a golden hue over the room, making it feel both intimate and inviting. I spotted my group of friends gathered around a large, circular table near the window, where the city lights twinkled like stars against the night sky.

Tiffany, with her vibrant naturally curly hair and infectious laugh, waved me over. Beside her sat Gavin, always impeccably dressed and quick with a witty remark. The rest of the group included Maya, a thoughtful and articulate lawyer; Jordan, a tech-savvy entrepreneur; Alex, a passionate environmentalist; Sam, a charismatic marketing executive; Leah, a talented graphic designer; and twins, Emma and Ethan, who were both in the finance sector.

As I joined them, the conversation was already in full swing, centered around the concept of "pretty privilege" in the workplace. It was a topic that sparked a lively debate, with opinions flying across the table. Half of the group believed it was a real phenomenon, while the other half dismissed it as a myth. I knew all too well that it existed, having experienced it firsthand throughout my career.

"Pretty privilege is definitely a thing," I said, my voice steady but firm. *"I've seen it play out in so many ways. Attractive people often get more opportunities, but it can also backfire. People assume you're less competent, and it becomes a double-edged sword."*

Maya nodded in agreement. *"It's true. I've seen it in the legal field as well. Attractive women are often underestimated, and their achievements are attributed to their looks rather than their skills."*

The conversation then shifted to the idea of "Pet to Threat," a phenomenon where a once-favored employee becomes a perceived threat to their superiors. I shared my own experience, recounting how I had been praised and supported in my last role, only to be sidelined and marginalized as I began to excel.

"It's like they want you to do well, but not too well," I explained. *"Once you start to outshine them, they see you as a threat rather than an asset."*

Jordan leaned forward; his expression thoughtful. *"It's frustrating how often that happens. It's like there's an invisible ceiling that you can't break through, no matter how hard you work."*

As the discussion continued, we delved into the broader issues of sexism, racism, and ageism in the workplace. Despite living in a supposedly progressive society, these biases still held sway, creating an uneven playing field for many talented individuals.

"Even in the most liberal environments, these biases exist," Leah pointed out. *"It's not just about talent or potential; it's about who fits the mold of what success is supposed to look like."*

Throughout the evening, I felt a sense of camaraderie with those who understood and supported my experiences. Yet, there were others who seemed to relish the idea of someone else's struggles, their skepticism evident in their dismissive comments.

"It's not always about bias," Sam argued. *"Sometimes people just aren't as good as they think they are."*

I took a deep breath, choosing my words carefully. *"It's not about thinking I'm better than anyone else. It's about recognizing the barriers that exist and working to overcome them. It's about being seen for my abilities, not just my appearance."*

The conversation was intense, but it was also semi-cathartic. I being emotionally pulled in two directions. For the first time, I felt somewhat comfortable discussing these issues openly, surrounded by people who, for the most part, understood the complexities of navigating a professional world fraught with challenges. At the same time, a chilling realization began to dawn on me, but it was too late to turn back.

As the night wore on, I realized that despite the setbacks and the injustices, I had survived and thrived in my own way. I had built a career, faced adversity, and continued to push forward, even when the odds were stacked against me.

Leaving the lounge, I felt a renewed sense of determination paired with an overwhelming feeling of defeat. The evening had been a whirlwind of emotions, and as I stepped out into the cool night air, the weight of the conversations lingered heavily on my shoulders. I had been powwowing with this group for four years now. While I wanted things to be fine, I wasn't completely sure I had the complete professional support of my *"friends"*. During the evening, there had been one too many side-eyes, and it left me a bit put off.

In the world of technological development, where innovation and expertise should be the only currencies that matter, I found myself entangled in a web of social dynamics that had little to do with my skills or accomplishments. As a young, beautiful African American woman, I had always been aware of the whispers of "pretty privilege" that followed me. It was a double-edged sword, one that cut deeper than most realized. On the one hand, my appearance often opened doors, granting me opportunities that might have been harder to come by otherwise. But on the other hand, it cast a shadow over my achievements, as if my looks somehow diminished the value of my hard-earned expertise and certifications.

The evening's gathering had been no different. As I mingled with the group, I could feel the undercurrents of resentment and jealousy. This had underscored the complexities of navigating social dynamics and professional challenges, particularly as a young African American woman in a competitive industry.

I shared the example of my previous supervisor, Karla, an older African American woman who had personally recruited me for my expertise in specific software. She initially presented herself as a mentor and ally. But over a short time, that budding relationship had shifted. What began as a nurturing dynamic had morphed into something more sinister —a classic case of "pet to threat." At first, she had championed my successes, parading me around as her protégé. But as I began to carve out my own niche, her support waned, replaced by a palpable tension.

Honestly, my career has always been a complicated dance of performance, ambition, and perception. I've spent years working to earn my place, building up certifications and expertise, proving I am more than my appearance. Yet, every time I step into a room, it feels like I have to navigate two versions of myself: the professional who knows her stuff and the one whose beauty seems to overshadow her credentials.

At first, it didn't bother me. I thought maybe I was just overthinking things, but the more I climbed the corporate ladder, the more I realized something wasn't right. Pretty privilege is supposed to be an advantage, right? It's supposed to be the sort of thing people envy, a tool that makes life easier. But in my experience, the opposite was true. Every compliment, every *"you're so beautiful"* or *"you've got that 'IT' factor,"* became a silent weapon aimed at undermining my professional accomplishments.

It wasn't just about the men who couldn't separate my looks from my capabilities. It was the way other women, particularly my peers, started treating me. Like I was a "pet" — someone cute and harmless, but never really worthy of being taken seriously. Karla had tracked me down through a recommendation and handpicked me for my current role. At first, I thought it was a compliment — maybe even an honor. She saw my potential, believed in my abilities, and recruited me into the high-pressure, male-dominated environment of tech development. She told me that I reminded her of herself when she was younger: smart, driven, and eager to prove my worth.

But the admiration, the support, it quickly soured into something more malevolent. The "pet to threat" dynamic was insidious, a silent battle waged in the corridors of power. Karla became both my biggest advocate and my sharpest critic, and it wasn't long before I realized her support came with strings attached. In meetings, she would praise me one minute for my work and the next minute suggest I *"tone down the charm"* or *"dress more conservatively,"* as if my wardrobe and my smile were the reasons for my success. She'd say things like, *"People are paying attention to your looks more than your work. Be careful, you don't want them thinking you got here because you're pretty."* It wasn't until I started facing subtle, then overt, exclusion that I realized what was happening.

Karla wasn't just a supervisor; she tried to use my brain as a tool to climb her own ladder. But once she realized the jig was up, that her leadership knew that it was me, that I was the rising star, she went into overdrive to make sure I didn't get to the top — or push me back down, if I did. I began to *feel* like I was a "pet," my skills just something to be paraded around, admired for a brief moment, and then put back in my place. I'd hear her tell others, *"She's talented, but she's a little too much of a distraction."* I began to feel like my career was being held hostage by a complex cocktail of envy and jealousy.

Exactly how my previous female supervisor had behaved years prior, it was as if my growth threatened her own standing, and rather than celebrate my achievements, she sought to contain them. The irony was not lost on me—two women of color, navigating a predominantly male industry, yet instead of lifting each other up, we were caught in a cycle of competition and mistrust.

To the group, I recalled a particular incident that encapsulated this ongoing turmoil. During a high-stakes project presentation, I had proposed an innovative solution that was met with unanimous enthusiasm by the senior leadership team—her supervisor *and his supervisors!* My supervisor, however, had been quick to undermine my contribution, subtly attempting to redirect the credit to herself. Although that endeavor backfired in her face in real time, it was a deft maneuver, one that left me questioning my own perceptions. Was she insane? How was she comfortable with *openly* making unprofessional, menacingly calculated moves aimed at keeping me in my place?

As I made it to my car, I reflected on the toll these dynamics had taken on my mental health. The constant need to prove myself, to validate my worth beyond my appearance, was exhausting. I had worked tirelessly to build a reputation based on merit, yet the specter of "pretty privilege" and the "pet to threat" transformation loomed large, casting doubt on my every success.

Once my work started really speaking for itself, once I started leading teams and receiving accolades, the same colleagues who had once praised me now treated me like I was competition. Karla's demeanor towards me started to shift too. Her once caring advice became passive-aggressive statements. *"Don't get too comfortable in that chair. You're not as irreplaceable as you think,"* she'd say, always with a knowing look in her eye. And when I tried to confront her, she dismissed me with a tight smile, as if I were overreacting. Eventually, Karla *was replaced* by her worst enemy in a shocking turn of events, but by then, I had already sustained my share of damage.

It was exhausting. I worked twice as hard to prove myself, but no matter what I did, the men in the room just saw me as the "pretty face." The women saw me as a threat. Everyone else saw me as a trophy, a pretty little thing who would never be truly respected for my brain and my ambition. My value had nothing to do with my skills and everything to do with the way I looked, and the way people were threatened by that.

Hoping to make my case solid, I also told the group about one particular project where I was the lead developer, a role that no one expected me to take on. I led the team with efficiency, making decisions based on logic, data, and my years of experience. But instead of recognizing my leadership, one of the senior developers, a man I had respected, pulled me aside and said, *"You know, you don't have to try so hard. Everyone knows why you're here. Just be pretty and let the rest fall into place."*

I didn't know what to say. I should've reported him. I should've called it out right then and there, but I didn't. Instead, I swallowed the words and worked even harder, trying to prove that I belonged in the room, even if no one seemed to think so. But the comments, the glances, the whispers—they never stopped.

What people didn't understand was that I was always walking a tightrope. I couldn't appear too capable, or I'd be seen as a threat. I couldn't appear too glamorous, or I'd be seen as a pet. Either way, I was destined to be someone's idea of what I should be, never allowed to simply be myself. Every step I took, every success I achieved, came at the cost of trying to fit into boxes that weren't built for me.

I started to realize that the higher I climbed, the more my identity was scrutinized. It wasn't just about the work anymore; it was about fitting into these preconceived molds of what a woman in tech should look like, act like, or be. I couldn't prevail.

Eventually, I learned that no amount of expertise could erase the judgments others placed on me. No certifications, no accolades, no projects I spearheaded could take away the fact that, as a young, beautiful, well qualified woman, I was constantly faced with the idea of being either an object of envy or a target of insecurity. Pretty privilege didn't work in my favor, and neither did being perceived as a threat. It was like I was caught in a game I wasn't ever allowed to win.

Sitting in my car, now ruminating, a little too distracted to pull out of my parking space, I replayed the discussions in my mind. The topic of "pretty privilege" had sparked a heated debate, and while I knew it existed, the dismissive attitudes of some in the group stung. It was as if my experiences were being invalidated, brushed aside as mere figments of my imagination. The skepticism in their eyes, the subtle smirks—it all felt like a betrayal. I had joined this group hoping to find camaraderie and understanding, but instead, I was now being met with doubt and derision.

The conversation about "Pet to Threat" had been no different. I thought about Dr. Kecia Thomas and her research on the "Pet to Threat" phenomenon. It was a relief to know that someone had put a name to what I was experiencing, that I wasn't alone in this struggle. But it was also a stark reminder of the systemic issues that still plagued industries like mine. I knew I had to keep pushing forward, not just for myself, but for the women who would come after me, who would face the same challenges and need someone to look up to. It was so unfortunate, though, as I shared my story, I noticed a few of them exchanging glances, as if silently questioning the validity of my experiences. It was disheartening, to say the least. I had opened up about a deeply personal struggle, only to be met with suspicion and judgment. It was a testament that not everyone in my circle had my best interests at heart.

As I drove home, the city lights blurring past, I couldn't shake the feeling of isolation. These were people I had considered friends, yet their reactions had left me questioning *everything*. Were they truly supportive, or were they secretly reveling in my struggles? The thought gnawed at me, fueling a growing sense of distrust.

I had always prided myself on my resilience, my ability to bounce back from adversity, regardless of how low I fell. But tonight, the cracks in my armor were beginning to show. The doubts and insecurities that I had managed to keep at bay were now threatening to overwhelm me. I couldn't help but wonder if my so-called friends were secretly hoping for my professional downfall, waiting for the moment when I would finally falter.

The realization was a bitter pill to swallow. I had been so focused on building my career, on proving myself in a world that often underestimated me, that I had overlooked the importance of genuine support. The thought of facing future challenges without a reliable support system was daunting, and it left me feeling more vulnerable than ever.

As I pulled into my driveway, the silence of the night enveloping me, I made a decision. I would no longer allow the negativity of others to dictate my self-worth. I would focus on surrounding myself with people who truly believed in me, who celebrated my successes and supported me through my failures. It was time to reevaluate my relationships and prioritize those who genuinely had my back.

But even as I resolved to make these changes, a lingering sense of unease remained. The seeds of doubt had been planted, and I knew it would take time to fully trust them again. For now, all I could do was take things one day at a time, holding onto the hope that brighter days were ahead.

Trevor

I've always found it a slight challenge to open up to people due to my anxiety and unstable self-esteem. I know there is no right or wrong level of being social, but I generally struggle with being around people altogether. Small talk seems so authentic and unnecessary to me. Maybe it's because of how I spent my entire childhood virtually in my own world? Perhaps it's due to me opening up, being vulnerable, and allowing someone in, only to have them hurt me deeply and unnecessarily? Personally, I think it's both, and the situation has been exacerbated by repeated events that have consistently pulled away at my soul.

Be that as it may, I still felt blessed because while my grandmother had proven thus far to be my greatest mentor and my one and only ride-or-die, I did have a good friend who I could count on to listen to me vent, as needed. His name was Trevor. We met a few years before college, during a summer program that brought together students from different high schools. Our friendship slowly blossomed over the next fifteen years. Trevor was the kind of person who could make anyone feel at ease. He had this infectious laugh and a way of looking at you that made you feel like you were the most important person in the room.

As a support system for each other, we would meet up a couple of times a month for food, drinks and routine venting. Trevor had been in a toxic relationship for the past four years, and while it was a source of stress for him, it never seemed to affect our friendship. We were always able to discuss the hot topic issues within his relationship, and I would provide helpful ways for him to manage it. I was not afraid of him; despite the challenges he faced in his relationship. Though there had been a few accusations of personal property damage between him and his ex, he was like a brother to me, someone I trusted implicitly, and someone I had no reason to fear.

At the time, he had just ended that unbalanced relationship, and I had been dealing with a lot of personal issues as of late, including the ongoing challenge of securing a less stressful job. I needed to see if he could help me unravel the evening I had just experienced. I needed to know if I should be concerned about the group, or if I were reading into things too much.

I remember it was an exciting time for me, though, because I had just recently met a potential suitor named Justin. It all started with a television food competition that I stumbled upon one Saturday evening. There he was this confident guy with a glint in his eye and a smile that could melt even the toughest critic. I don't typically watch these kinds of shows, but Justin had such a magnetic presence on screen. He won first place, naturally, and I thought to myself, *"well, he's not only talented, but he's also actually pretty attractive too."*

I didn't expect anything to come of it, but on a whim, I decided to email him. *"Congrats on the win, Justin! Your dish looked amazing, and you totally deserved first place. I hope to see you on TV again soon!"* I sent it off, probably overthinking the whole thing. But the next morning, my inbox lit up with a reply from him. It was short, sweet, and genuine. *"Thanks so much! Appreciate it! Hope you're doing well!"* It was simple, but it was a spark. We started talking more, and before I knew it, we were chatting every day.

He made me laugh more than I could have imagined. We talked about everything—his experiences on the show, his passion for food, even his dog, which he often joked was the real star of his show. And then there was the constant back-and-forth of bad puns and food-related jokes. One of my favorites came from him one evening, when we were chatting about pizza. He sent me a message saying, *"Why did the pizza go to the party alone? Because it knew how to 'cheese' the crowd!"* I groaned and laughed at the same time, thinking to myself that this was a man who understood how to make light of even the simplest things. I couldn't help but laugh at how ridiculous it was, but also how perfect it was. That's when I decided to reply with my own: *"Okay, well, what did the lettuce say to the celery at the party?*

'Lettuce romaine friends!'" He let out an immediate laugh, clearly entertained. We both knew it was cheesy—pun intended—but it was exactly that kind of silly humor that made me look forward to every conversation with him.

Our conversations naturally shifted to deeper topics, too. I was surprised when he asked if he could call me one day. It felt like a big step, but I said yes. Our first call was hours long, and at the end of it, he casually mentioned, *"By the way, I've spoken to my mom about you. She's excited to meet you!"* Wait, what? His mom? I was taken aback at first, but soon enough, I found myself talking to his mom over the phone. She was warm and welcoming, chatting with me like we'd known each other for years. Apparently, Justin had told her all about me, and she wanted to make sure I knew just how much she supported this whole thing.

We had been talking for about three months now and were preparing to meet for the first time in Atlanta on New Year's Eve.

Trevor and I met at our usual spot, a cozy little bar tucked away in a quiet corner of the city, not far from our respective neighborhoods. The dim lighting and soft music provided the perfect backdrop for our conversations. As I walked in, I spotted him at our usual table, nursing a drink and scrolling through his phone.

He looked up as I approached, flashing me a warm smile.

"Hey, you," he greeted, standing up to give me a hug. *"How's it going?"*

I sighed, taking a seat across from him. *"It's been a day,"* I admitted, running a hand through my hair. *"I had this meeting with my professional group, and it just left me feeling... off."*

Trevor raised an eyebrow, taking a sip of his drink. *"Off how?"*

I hesitated, trying to find the right words. *"I don't know. There were just a lot of side-eyes and whispers. It felt like they were judging me, you know? Like they were waiting for me to fail. Kinda like they might be enjoying the challenges that I'm dealing with in my office."*

He nodded; his expression thoughtful. *"Young, no kids, beautiful home, strong savings, impressive career, 842 credit score, killer skills in the kitchen — Do you think they're jealous of your success?"*

"Maybe," I admitted. *"But it just made me feel so insecure. Like, I can't even trust the people who are supposed to be my friends."*

Trevor reached across the table, giving my hand a reassuring squeeze. *"Hey, don't let them get to you. You're beautiful, you're smart, you're amazing, hella sexy and anyone who can't see that isn't worth your time."* With that, I wondered if Trevor had misspoken, but I decided not to request clarification. The evening had indeed been stressful, so maybe I had just misheard him.

As he continued to speak, his words were semi-comforting, and I felt a little of the tension ease from my shoulders. *"Thanks, Trevor. I don't know what I'd do without you."*

He grinned, leaning back in his chair. *"That's what I'm here for. So, tell me more about this Justin guy. Are you excited to meet him?"*

I felt a smile tug at my lips at the mention of Justin. *"Yeah, I am. We've been talking for a while now, and he seems really great. I'm just nervous, you know? What if he doesn't like me in person?"*

Trevor chuckled, shaking his head. *"Trust me, he's going to love you. You're a catch."*

_____

As the night wore on, the earlier tension slowly melted away. We spent the rest of the night talking and laughing, the camaraderie among us growing stronger with each shared story. Trevor had a way of making everything seem okay, even when it wasn't. His presence was a comforting reminder that I wasn't alone in my struggles.

Feeling relaxed and content, I realized that the evening had been a success, after all. I had been able to count on Trevor once again, and it was reassuring to know that our friendship remained as strong as ever.

Throughout the night, I had been exchanging text messages with Justin. Our conversation was lighthearted and flirtatious, filled with the kind of private jokes and innuendos that made my heart race. Trevor was aware of my texting, but he never let on that he was jealous or annoyed. He simply smiled and continued to engage, his easygoing nature putting me at ease.

By now, it was after 11 p.m., and I was feeling the effects of the incredibly long evening. Tired and ready to head home, I left my unlocked cell phone on the table and excused myself to the restroom while Trevor called for the check. When I returned, Trevor informed me that he had taken care of the bill and that we were good to go. I thanked him, grateful for his generosity, and we made our way outside.

Once outside the restaurant, Trevor turned to me with a hopeful expression. *"I'm actually not ready to go home yet,"* he admitted, his voice tinged with a hint of pleading. *"How about we go to another place for just one more drink? I know it's late, but I really want to treat you to a mojito at your favorite spot."*

I hesitated, the thought of my cozy bed calling to me, but Trevor's earnestness was hard to resist. Reluctantly, I agreed, knowing that he had always been there for me when I needed him. Trevor insisted that I get into his car, promising that we could retrieve my car later. Trusting him implicitly, I climbed into the passenger seat, and we headed to the second restaurant.

As we drove through the quiet streets, I couldn't help but feel a sense of gratitude for Trevor's friendship. He had been a constant in my life, a source of support and understanding. Little did I know that this night would mark the beginning of the greatest betrayal I would ever experience. But at that moment, I was blissfully unaware, content in the knowledge that I had a friend I could trust with my life.

As Trevor and I stepped into the nearly deserted restaurant, the quiet atmosphere felt oddly comforting. It was a stark contrast to the lively chatter of the previous place we'd been. I slid into a booth in the bar area, my mind still buzzing with excitement from my ongoing conversation with Justin. The anticipation of our upcoming meet-up had me in high spirits, and I was barely aware of Trevor as he made his way to the bar to order drinks.

When he returned with a mojito for me and nothing for himself, I raised an eyebrow. *"Why didn't you get a drink?"* I asked, half-jokingly. *"If you weren't going to drink, then why on earth did we come here? You're weird to me."*

Trevor chuckled softly, assuring me that he simply enjoyed my company and didn't want to head home just yet, especially after his recent breakup. I nodded, accepting his explanation, and returned my attention to my phone, my fingers dancing over the screen as I continued texting Justin.

Minutes passed, and Trevor pointed out that I hadn't touched my drink. I hesitated, not really in the mood for alcohol, but took a sip anyway to be polite. The mojito tasted normal, but after a couple more sips, I felt a strange sensation creeping over me. My vision blurred slightly, and my balance felt off as I stood up to head to the restroom.

Inside the bathroom, I stumbled into the stall door with a loud bang, startling myself. Everything seemed distorted, as if I were floating. Panic bubbled up inside me. This wasn't the usual effect of a mojito, especially not from this bar. I managed to use the restroom, albeit clumsily, and washed my hands, trying to steady my racing thoughts.

As I reached for the bathroom door handle, I gasped in surprise. Trevor was standing right there, concern etched on his face. *"Why are you doing?"* I slurred, struggling to form the words.

"I heard the loud bang and wanted to make sure you were okay," he replied smoothly. *"We're leaving."*

"No!" I protested, my voice shaky. *"I have to get my cell phone and my wallet from the booth."*

Trevor reassured me with a calm demeanor that he already had my belongings and that we were indeed headed for the car. His words barely registered as I tried to process the situation, my mind clouded and sluggish. A part of me knew something was terribly wrong, but I couldn't quite grasp it.

As he guided me out of the restaurant and to his car, I knew I would NOT be able to drive my own car tonight. I could barely hold my head up! The cool night air hit my face, a stark contrast to the warm, dimly lit restaurant we had just left. Trevor, ever the gentleman, opened the passenger door of his sleek, black sedan for me. I sank into the plush leather seat, grateful for the support as I tried to gather my scattered thoughts.

The car's interior was immaculate, the faint scent of new leather mingling with Trevor's subtle cologne. As he started the engine, the dashboard lights flickered to life, casting a soft glow that seemed to blur at the edges of my vision. I leaned back, closing my eyes for a moment, trying to steady the spinning world around me.

Trevor pulled out of the parking lot, and we began our short journey to my house. The streets were eerily quiet, the usual hustle and bustle of the city replaced by an almost serene stillness. It was 11:35 p.m., and it seemed as though the world had gone to sleep, leaving just the two of us to navigate the empty roads.

As we approached the first stoplight, I tried to focus on Trevor's voice. He was talking, his words a steady stream of sound, but I couldn't make sense of them. It was as if he were speaking a language I had never heard before, each syllable slipping through my mind like water through a sieve. I nodded occasionally, hoping it was the right response, but I couldn't be sure.

The second stoplight came and went, the car gliding smoothly through the intersection. I watched the city lights blur past the window, their colors blending into a kaleidoscope of reds, greens, and yellows. My head felt heavy, and I fought the urge to close my eyes again, knowing that sleep would only make the nausea worse.

As we neared the third stoplight, a sudden wave of heat washed over me, my skin prickling with an uncomfortable warmth. My heart raced, a fight-or-flight response triggered by the alcohol coursing through my veins. I tried to take a deep breath, but it was too late. The contents of my stomach surged upward, and before I could stop it, I was vomiting all over the pristine interior of Trevor's car.

I was mortified, my cheeks burning with shame as I wiped my mouth with the back of my hand. Trevor glanced over at me, his expression calm and unbothered. *"That's okay,"* he said softly, his voice reassuring. *"We're almost at your house."*

His lack of concern for the mess I had made was both comforting and unsettling. I knew how much he valued his car, and yet he seemed unfazed by the disaster I had just created. It was an indictment of his character.

We pulled up to my house, the familiar sight of my front porch a welcome relief. Trevor parked the car and helped me out, his hand steadying me as I fumbled with my keys. I managed to unlock the door, leaving the keys dangling in the lock as I stumbled inside.

I barely registered Trevor's presence as I made my way upstairs, my only goal to wash away the remnants of the night. The bathroom light was harsh, reflecting off the tiles as I turned on the shower. I stepped into my walk-in closet, struggling to undress. My boots were a challenge, the straps refusing to cooperate, and I sat on the floor in defeat.

Trevor appeared in the doorway; his expression was one of concern. *"Are you okay?"* he asked, kneeling beside me. I nodded, though I wasn't sure if it was true. He offered to help, and I gratefully accepted, watching as he deftly removed the stubborn boots.

With his assistance, I managed to shed the rest of my clothes, my embarrassment nearly overshadowed by gratitude. I felt exposed, vulnerable, but Trevor's presence, helping me whilst I was very sick, was a comfort. He left the bathroom as I stepped into the shower, the water washing away the night's mistakes.

I emerged, wrapping myself in a towel without bothering to properly dry myself off. My mind was a haze, the world outside my bedroom a distant concern. I collapsed onto my bed, the cool down comforter a welcome relief against my skin. The door was open, but I didn't care. I was home, and that was all that mattered.

As I drifted into unconsciousness, I was vaguely aware of Trevor's footsteps retreating down the stairs. I didn't know if he would stay or go, but at that moment, it didn't matter. I was safe, and for now, that was enough.

———————

CHAPTER SIX

TRANSCENDENCE

"When we are no longer able to change a situation, we are challenged to change ourselves."
— *Viktor Frankl*

It's very beautiful here. From my wraparound balcony there are so many amazingly majestic panoramic views of the city and mountains that will steal your breath away. The atmosphere in and around Pacifique Peak is always so serene and fresh.

Taking my time to pull it in deeply, the crisp, clean air fills my lungs, energizes me and clears my eyes. It refreshes my body and mind and generally gives me a heightened sense that I am alive.

It all feels humbling to me.

Moving here a year ago was strategic with the goal of me reshaping my reality. During one of my counseling sessions, I learned new ways to improve my mental health. After a shallow discussion about the traumas that I have experienced over my life, I was introduced to the idea that our brains constantly rewire themselves to suit the information that is fed into it. Constant complaining, gossiping, finding excuses, etc., will make it much easier for the mind to find things to be upset about, regardless of what is actually happening around you. Likewise, if you constantly search for opportunities, abundance, love, and things to be grateful for, it will make it much easier to find a reflection of those things around you. I was told that while it takes practice and consistency, over time, intentional positivity is a very powerful way to rewire your brain, essentially reshaping your reality.

I left that counseling session and called my supervisor as soon as I got into my car:

"This job has taken me completely off balance. I'll be taking an emergency leave of absence, effective immediately."

Once home, I quickly packed a bag and readied myself for an impromptu road trip.

With Chattanooga, Tennessee programmed into my GPS, I soon entered the freeway. I-64W.

It's perfect here. The lake view affords me a particular peace because of the memories it keeps. I oftentimes find myself gazing out ahead, exhaling slowly to expel the tension while casting my worries and doubts into the shallow blue water. Reclaiming my peace.

To behold the beauty of it all calms my soul and I wish I could capture the feeling of the peacefulness in a bottle. I would always have it with me in my many times of fear or discomfort.

In the distance surrounding the lake's edge are a beautiful variety of trees lightly swaying back and forth. This evening, the water is calm and it's impossible to feel anything but tranquility. It's perfect here.

I love to come out at dusk as the sun is setting behind the mountain. Hearing the wind music of the trees gives me an immediate sense of equanimity. The entrancing sound rapidly relaxes me in a way that is indescribable.

Typically, the day begins and ends with me spending time out here thinking and breathing and thinking and breathing some more. Meditating has been a blessing in that it allows me to restore my energy.

In a great example of irony, I've organized this evening for myself as a celebration of life. Complete with a little spread of my favorite things, foods and fruits, I can hear my music playing softly in the background.

Before I moved here, music was my only peace. After a stressful day in the toxic work environment with Karla, I would often find myself in a deep valley with sadness and anxiety quickly pouring into my soul. A familiar song would come on my heart and trigger hope. Immediately, I would take action and within a minute or two, I'd be listening to the inspiriting song, loudly, with the anxiety and sadness rapidly transforming into calmness and joy.

For me, music is a medicine delivered in the most divine way as the lyrics swim through my soul to the sounds of the relaxing notes. Music blesses my cerebral cortex by teaching my brain to relax and be at peace. A lifetime of learning, yet only now I've come to realize that you won't be able to find peace, you have to cultivate it.

Now, after many long days and short moments of intentional focus and asking God to calm my mind, heal my heart and take my worries away, I have a new peace as the view of the lake instantly calms my soul.

In the distance, I can see the slight movement of the tree branches as I hear a gentle swishing sound of the leaves rustling in the wind. A light breeze passes over me and I am triggered. I suddenly recall a day that has been hell to forget.

Quickly diverting my thoughts, with eyes and mouth closed, I remind myself to slow down. *"Two, three, four..."*, I say in my mind. With this four-count slow and deep inhale through my nose, I can feel the air filling up my lungs. I pause and hold the air inside for another count of four. Then, I start a slow, six-count exhaling through my mouth.

I use this breathing technique to clear my mind and recenter myself. In this moment, I'm desperately trying, but the stain is still coming through. Staving off a panic attack, I continue doing the breathing exercise, repeatedly. Count after count. I want tonight to be peaceful, and I want to be composed.

My eyes gloss over with tears as I remember lying there, bare, with water droplets on my skin. The ceiling fan was on, and the swirling wind gave my incapacitated body a deep chill.

Things went downhill fast after that. I never made it to Atlanta. The excitement I once felt about seeing Justin for the first time on New Year's Eve was replaced by a heavy, suffocating weight. When I called to explain why I couldn't make the trip, I hoped for understanding, maybe even a little comfort. Instead, his words cut deeper than I could have imagined.

"You're not the first person to go through something like this, and you won't be the last," he said, his voice devoid of

empathy. *"Just get over it and come in two weeks."*

I was stunned. The person I thought I could lean on, who I had shared so much with, was now dismissing my pain as if it were a mere inconvenience. It was as if the trauma I had endured was nothing more than a blip on his radar, something to be brushed aside for the sake of his own desires.

The call ended, leaving me in a silence that felt louder than any noise. I sat there, phone in hand, feeling the walls close in around me. The heartbreak was twofold: the loss of Trevor, who had been like a brother, and now Justin, who I thought could be something more. I felt a profound sense of loss, not just of people, but of my own self-respect.

I had no idea the sheer capacity of damage that could be inflicted by one person's selfish actions. Imagine the weight I was under from *two* people's selfish actions. How to survive a figurative stab in your heart — It was a lesson I never wanted to learn, but one that would stay with me forever.

Healing is hard. We oftentimes hear about being resilient, but rarely are we taught just how much effort it takes to hold on to hope, to get back up, and to try once again. I've come so far in the past year yet there's still so far to go. If I have learned anything, I know for certain that life leads us on many journeys that we would not go on if it were up to us.

A person can look happy and still be miserable inside. I accomplished this plenteousness life but was always so dispirited that I had failed to truly be proud of myself. Despite the consistent reminders and powerful teachings of my grandmother, somehow I still managed to naively place all my value at the mercy of others.

Tonight, for the first time in my life, I'm owning this truth.

Alone in the darkness, save for a few persistent embers in the fire pit and some fireflies off in the distance, I slowly meet me. I'm realizing who I am and accepting who I am not.

So many beautiful pieces came together to become the essence of me. Accountable, brave, educated, hardworking, influential, patient, reliable, successful and thoughtful. I'm compassionate with others, and I treat obstacles as steppingstones on my way to my goals.

To those looking in, I'm so impressive that young girls emulate me, hoping to be like me when they grow up. The role my grandma played in my development has been essential to my self-presentation. Yet still, I struggle with feeling good about myself.

In the background I see a firefly light up. I remember all the times I used to scurry around the backyard at dusk chasing and capturing them. Shifting my focus, I admire the spread that I put out, refreshments and crudités consisting of my favorite party foods. I have a cheese and cracker tray, a fruit tray, fresh vegetables, desserts and a pitcher of sangria.

"How did I get here?", I ask myself.

It was a simple, sunny day in late May when I heard the news. Grandma had been released from the hospital but would be introduced to hospice care. The doctors determined that her illness had progressed to the point where treatments could no longer control it. We needed to understand that she was in the final stages of her life.

I wasn't ready. But there was no other choice. For the next three months, I made sure to call Momo every day, and I went by the house as often as I could. I made video recordings of her and saved every voicemail that she left. I asked her to re-tell many of the stories I've heard her tell dozens of times. I entered grief counseling to get assistance with developing methods and strategies for coping with my loss. I had never felt that way before, so I knew I would need a licensed professional to help me find ways to come to terms with my new reality. I did all I could to get ready, but even today, over two years later, I'm still not ready.

When I got the call from her nurse, I was in Los Angeles for work. Hearing that she may not make it through the night, I stopped everything that I was doing and contacted the airline to change my flights. My ticket to fly home on Friday would need to be moved up to *now*.

There was nothing available that afternoon, but I was able to get on the first flight the next morning. Drowning in my emotions I made it back to my hotel room and called a friend. I shared that the time had come, and grandma would be transitioning soon.

During the call with my friend, I mentioned that I had tried to reach Momo all day, but didn't get any response. Desperately attempting to convince myself that everything was totally fine, I explained that it was probably simply because she's been resting.

Appreciating the focused attention and compassionate, non-alarmist attitude that she was giving, I took time to express my regret for taking this work trip in the first place. It felt like the biggest mistake I had ever made, and I couldn't help but feel the weight of it with every passing moment. My original schedule had me home, on vacation this week—finally taking a much-needed break from the chaos of work, a break that I had planned around Momo. I was supposed to be there with her, spending time together in what I knew were our final moments. The days I had left to be with her were precious, and I couldn't afford to waste them.

When I got the news that she was nearing the end, I made arrangements to come home, canceling all work commitments, everything, to make sure I could be there with her. But then came the request to take this work trip—an unimportant, routine trip that should have been easy to reschedule. My boss, a woman who had no real empathy for anyone, especially not for family matters, wasn't willing to make an exception.

It broke my heart to have to call Momo and give her the update that I was having to push my trip home back another week. I had promised her I would be there, I had told her I would drop everything, yet now I had to break that promise. She'd always been my rock, the one who had taught me about strength and love and unconditional care. She deserved better than this. She deserved to have me by her side, not in some hotel room on the other side of the country, stuck in a job that never seemed to understand how human life works.

To be clear, the work situation was very simple—it was an unfortunate result of having a boss who was an insensitive, controlling, narcissistic bitch. She was the type who had no limits, no understanding of what it meant to be compassionate. She saw the world through a lens of self-interest, and her manipulation extended beyond just office politics. When I put in my personal leave request, explaining that I needed time to go spend time with my sick grandmother, she knew exactly what was going on. But that didn't matter to her. She had no regard for what I was going through. She still assigned me to this trip, a trip that, in the grand scheme of things, had no minor or major implications for the company.

This wasn't a matter of some emergency situation where the

company would be in jeopardy without me—no, it was simply a project that could have been handled at a later time. But instead, she forced me, with complete disregard for my personal circumstances, to reschedule my time off.

Her rationale was simple: the job was always the priority, no matter what. Family, health, personal matters—none of that mattered when it came to her demands. She saw people as tools, expendable, and her own needs and power came first. My grandma's condition wasn't her problem, and she didn't seem to care that every moment I spent away from her felt like a moment I couldn't get back. Momo was my heart, my lifeline, and there was no way to explain to her that I wasn't there when she needed me most. No amount of work deadlines could ever compare to the urgency of being with someone you love during their final days.

And so, I did what I always did—I gave in. I rescheduled my time off, pushing my return home back a week. I complied with the demands, even though I knew it wasn't right, even though I knew deep down that I should have stood up for myself. It was never easy to say no to her, not when she had such a way of making you feel like you were disposable. But this time, it hurt more than ever before. The price of my compliance wasn't just another missed deadline or another unpaid overtime hour. This time, the price was Momo.

Now, I regret it deeply. I regretted not standing my ground, not refusing to let someone so emotionally disconnected control my personal life. I hated myself for thinking that the company's need for a few more reports or meetings could outweigh the need for me to be with the woman who had shaped me, who had loved me, and who was now slipping away.

This work trip was not a matter of life or death for the company—it was just another task in an endless line of tasks. But my trip home to visit my grandmother? That *was* life or death. I needed to be there to say goodbye, to hold her hand, to offer her the love and comfort she had always given me. And yet, here I was, caught between a company that didn't care and a personal loss that was too immense to bear alone. My boss, with her cold and calculated nature, had made it impossible for me to choose what mattered most, and I was paying the price.

That night, I slept just enough to allow my heart palpitations to slow down some.

In the morning, I was up and dressed with the scattered attention of a nervous child on the first day of school. I was so glad to be able to get on the first flight as time was not on my side. Based on what the nurse had cautioned, technically, I had already run out of time but resolved to remain hopeful that Momo would still be alert and oriented when I made it to her.

Ready to head out, I requested a ride to the airport and did a final check of the room. Luggage in tow, I picked up my phone and saw a new message:

"Call me."

"Momo died about an hour ago."

My brothers' words sounded like sharp razors slicing up my soul. I could barely hear his words through the fog of disbelief that clouded my mind.

"Huh?", I asked. *"She's gone?!"*

But when the reality finally broke through, my heart sank. *"She's gone,"* he said, and I felt the weight of those two words crush me.

I could barely respond. My mind was spinning. My grandmother, the one constant in my life, the one who raised me and gave me the strength to face everything, was gone.

"Okay, I'm here," my brother continued, his voice steady despite the gravity of what he had just told me. *"I've already called June and David. They're on their way. I'll take care of the funeral home, don't worry about that. And I'll handle the death certificate and the paperwork with the doctor. I know what needs to be done."*

I could hear him take a breath before adding, *"You don't need to deal with this right now. Just focus on getting here, okay? We'll take care of everything else."*

In a haze, I nodded, even though he couldn't see me. But I didn't trust myself to speak, not with the flood of emotions threatening to take over. The world seemed to shift beneath me, everything around me suddenly out of focus. I knew there were things to do, practical things. But right now, it felt like there was nothing to do but hold on to the reality that my grandmother was gone.

I listened to him as he kept talking, as if his calm voice was the only anchor in the storm I felt inside. He was already stepping up—making those difficult calls to the funeral home, ensuring the right people would be notified, and taking care of the details that felt too much to handle at this moment. But I couldn't shake the feeling that all the plans in the world didn't matter. My heart had shattered in an instant, and no amount of logistics could fix that.

I filled him in on the latest happenings with my flights and my tentative arrival schedule and I let him know that I was on my way to the airport. I grabbed the box of Kleenex from the bathroom counter and headed to the elevator.

As I approached the front desk, all was good. I was in control, poised, and upright. I let the front desk clerk know that I was checking out earlier than planned and that I would need a printed receipt. He prepared the receipt and asked me how my stay was.

Then, I lost it.

———

CHAPTER SEVEN

CONVERGENCE

"You may not control all the events that happen to you, but you can decide not to be reduced by them."
— Maya Angelou

The weeks following the death of my grandmother were nothing more than ebbs and flows of me 'losing it' and then trying to get myself under control. The first four weeks I stayed in bed. I never left my place once. I hardly ate food, drank water, showered or brushed my teeth. I just cried and slept and slept and cried. It was the real deal. I'd never experienced anything else remotely as painful as this before and it was incredibly difficult to navigate.

Hoping to see a way out of this darkness, I intentionally recalled some of my teachings from grief counseling. I started with my breathing exercises and worked myself up to repeating some positive affirmations. I began journaling heavily and was able to release many of the feelings that were rotting inside me. The feelings that were planted and nurtured by my heartless boss.
Thankfully, my journal was a safe place. It felt so invigorating to be able to reveal my private feelings and mean, incredibly

disrespectful thoughts, without judgment or punishment.

Eventually, I became strong enough to desire fellowship. Several of my local acquaintances were aware that I had sustained a great loss a few weeks earlier. Even though they had barely reached out to me, I knew that I would need them to help me heal.

I needed them badly. They each failed me.

They'll probably never know the strength it took for me to reach out to them and invite them to have dinner with me. It was such a critical time, and I was doing my utmost to *feel* again.

One of the most helpful things a person can do to see themselves through depression is to find a strong support circle and spend time with the people they love. Although this might seem easy, it's one of the hardest things to do, especially when your circle doesn't have the time or the interest in supporting you.

Losing someone you love can be one of the most painful experiences you'll ever have to endure. The level of support you have around you, your personality, and your own levels of health and well-being can all play a role in how grief impacts you following bereavement. It's important that we all know and understand this so we can carefully and intentionally make time to be available when someone in our circle needs us.

Grief is hard. Being completely blown off by everyone in my circle left me reeling, so I embarked upon the journey of my life, solo. Although I'd been pulling myself up out of dark places since I was a child, I would always have my grandma to speak encouraging words to me. I lived my life to make her proud. Now that she was gone, I regularly struggled with knowing my purpose for living.

As the weeks went on, I was able to stay somewhat motivated and go out to gatherings when I was invited. Fighting the urge to isolate, I made myself go to brunches and happy hours and shows and celebrations with the same people who ignored me when I needed them the most. Being a supportive friend trending towards death on the inside, I silently held myself together as best I could on the outside—of that, I was proud. I was trying. But I still struggled, nonetheless.

After months of struggling, my faith began to waiver. The intensity of my job became too much to bear and was causing me to lose my grip on the internal war I was fighting. I was working so hard to be ok. I was incorrectly calculating just how much stress my work was generating, hindering my personal progress.

When I went to a routine doctor's appointment and learned that my kidneys were on the verge of failing, I knew I had to take severe, immediate action. Things had gotten too far out of control. I had been under constant stress for *years*, juggling typically toxic work, personal issues, and the pressure of everyday life. What I didn't realize was how stress was silently wreaking havoc on my body, particularly my kidneys.

As it turns out, chronic stress triggers the release of stress hormones like cortisol, which, over time, can cause inflammation in various organs. The kidneys, which are responsible for filtering waste from the blood, can become compromised by this inflammation. When inflammation builds up, it can damage the kidneys' delicate filtering system, leading to reduced function and, in severe cases, kidney failure. My doctor explained that stress-induced inflammation had put unnecessary strain on my kidneys, weakening them and affecting their ability to function properly.

The worst part? I had ignored the signs for so long—dizziness, fatigue, headaches, blurred vision and unstable blood pressure—

thinking they were just part of the perpetual stress. My doctor's consistently failing to take my concerns seriously. Now, I'm making drastic lifestyle changes to manage my stress levels, including practicing mindfulness, exercising regularly, and adopting a healthier diet. It's a daily commitment, but I know my kidneys—and my overall health—depend on it. That year had been much too much, and I was done.

Moving to a new city in the mountains was my new lease of life. For me, starting over in a new city where I don't know anyone is exhilarating. When I move to a new place, every moment of every day brings a sense of discovery and surprise. New people! New restaurants! New smells and sights and sounds! I revel in this constant stream of novelty.

On my second day in Chattanooga, I found a home that I fell in love with! It was a spectacular, move-in ready, newly renovated six-bedroom home in the heart of Pacifique Peak with convenient access to Meade Hills and downtown. The breathtaking grand foyer with 3 story elliptical staircase flanked by embassy sized rooms was impressive! It featured hardwood floors throughout, a gourmet kitchen with east and west views just off the formal dining room, remodeled baths and a master on the main level. The spa-like owner's bath featured a steam shower, jetted tub, heated floor and anti-fog mirrors! The home had a neutral color palette throughout and was set on three secluded acres of beautifully landscaped grounds. It had a new heated pool, spa, custom decking, outdoor kitchen and a fire pit.

I could picture myself enjoying the sunrise from the sunroom with easy access to the deck and backyard. I could relax in the evenings viewing the sunset from the large covered front porch or living room. The amazing home also had a finished lower level opening to the large, gated parking area, 3+ car garage.

There was an irrigation system and lighting in the expansive yard. Although my social life was shaky, it was still a great place for entertaining family and friends! Captivated in a transformative sense, I quickly put in an offer.

My mind trails off to recollect days of the past and I lock into the memories that shaped my journey. Growing up in that small town, I always felt like a big fish in a tiny pond, yearning for the vast ocean beyond. The streets were lined with familiar faces and places, each corner holding memories of a simpler time. Yet, in my young, creative mind, I believed that leaving was my only chance of survival.

I remember the long summer days spent lying in the grass, staring up at the sky, imagining the life I would lead once I broke free from the confines of that town. I dreamed of bustling cityscapes, towering skyscrapers, and the hum of opportunity that seemed to pulse through the air in places far from here. Success, to me, was synonymous with escape.

My parents, though supportive, never quite understood my urgency to leave. They were content with the rhythm of life in Forte Le Coeur, finding joy in the small things that I often overlooked. But I was determined. I poured myself into my studies, convinced that education was my ticket out. I spent countless nights at the local library, devouring books that transported me to worlds beyond my own.

As I grew older, my dreams only intensified. I wanted to make a name for myself, to prove that I could rise above the limitations of my small-town upbringing. I envisioned a life where I could be anyone I wanted to be, unburdened by the expectations and judgments of those who had known me since childhood.

Now, as I sit here in the chill of the night, I realize that while I did leave Forte Le Coeur and achieved a measure of success, the town never truly left me. It shaped me in ways I hadn't anticipated, grounding me with a sense of identity and belonging that I only came to appreciate once I was far from its borders. The dreams of my youth were not just about leaving; they were about finding my place in the world, a journey that began so many years ago.

Cheddar trots onto the patio and nudges my leg, pulling me out of my reminiscent thoughts.

Once the sale was complete and I had the keys to my new home, I finally felt at ease enough to open up about my excitement and plans for the future. In good taste, I enthusiastically shared the exciting news with my friends. Their responses were less than adequate for the greater need.

I remember being semi-embarrassed when Gavin was the only person who said, *"Congratulations!"* Leaving the meet-up that day was extra painful. Too pissed to move, I sat in my car for a moment longer, the engine idling softly as I tried to gather my thoughts. The memory of that night at the lounge, and the tepid response from the professional's group, lingered in my mind like a shadow. It was as if their recent lack of enthusiasm had reopened an old wound, one that I had tried so hard to heal. I had shared my plans for the future, my excitement about the new house, hoping for a spark of joy or encouragement. Instead, their lukewarm responses felt like a dismissal, a reminder of the night I left the lounge feeling unseen and unheard.

My memory and recollections of events have always been stellar. In a split second, it was as if I was back in that moment, my heart heavy with the weight of unspoken words and unacknowledged pain.

I struggled to understand why things were going so badly with the people who I had chosen to be my friends. Did they not realize how much stress my soul was dealing with? I had to acknowledge my own role in this ongoing misunderstanding and accept that I had been preventing them from having a solid chance at fully knowing me. Perhaps their perceived lack of concern for me was just them growing fatigued with their filtered positions in my life?

Perhaps...?

In reflecting on my recent experiences, I've come to realize that perhaps my friends didn't simply abandon me during my time of need. Instead, I might not have been the best friend to them, which could have led to their dismissive behavior when I needed them the most. I've learned that relationships require clear communication, honesty, and courage to be vulnerable. Without these elements, I wasn't giving our friendships a fair chance to thrive. I see now that my failure to communicate openly and honestly during my greatest moments of need may have contributed to the distance that grew between us. This self-awareness has taught me the importance of being accountable for my energy and actions in any relationship.

That night after the lounge, I had made a decision that would haunt me for years. Put off by the events that evening, I chose not to tell them what happened later, not to share the new darkness that had crept into my life. I was torn between wanting to be understood and not wanting to ruin a man's life. Trevor was someone I had trusted, someone I thought I knew. But the events of that night shattered that illusion, leaving me with a secret too heavy to bear alone.

In the days, weeks, months and years that followed, I tried to convince myself that I could handle it. I believed, erroneously, that I could compartmentalize the trauma, lock it away in a corner of my mind and move on. But the poison seeped into every aspect of my life, slowly killing me from the inside, nearly decimating my kidneys.

Unbeknownst to me, I was living with high-functioning depression, going through the motions of daily life while feeling hollow and disconnected. For years following the incident, I attributed my feelings to the hostile work environments, stress or fatigue, not realizing the depth of my mental health issues. I was surviving, but I was not thriving.

The nightmares were relentless, vivid and terrifying, leaving me gasping for breath in the middle of the night. In them, Trevor was always there, a looming presence that I couldn't escape. I would wake up drenched in sweat, my heart racing, unable to shake the feeling of dread. The anxiety spilled over into my waking life, coloring my interactions with *all* men, making me question their intentions and my own judgment.

I struggled with a profound lack of self-worth, doubting every decision I made, every word I spoke. Trust became an elusive concept, something I couldn't extend to others or even to myself.

Eventually, once I began to suspect that I might be suffering on a clinical level, the stigma surrounding mental health issues led me to hide my depression. I feared judgment or repercussions at work, so I put on a brave face and continued to perform well.

In my social circle, I practiced isolation. I skipped out on some of the group activities, but I tried to make sure everyone saw me regularly…enough. I became adept at maintaining a social facade— made sure to smile, engage in small talk, and appear cheerful, making it difficult for others to truly see my internal pain.

Then, my physical health began to deteriorate, a reflection of the turmoil within. I overcompensated at work, throwing myself into projects with a fervor that bordered on obsession, trying to prove to myself and the world that I was still capable, still in control. There was an internalized pressure to succeed and not let others down, which drove me to push through my depression to meet expectations.

But beneath the surface, I was crumbling. I was unsure of my friends, unsure of myself, unsure of my health, trapped in a cycle of fear, silence and self-doubt. Since day one, I knew that if I reported Trevor, it would ruin his life, his career, his future. And so, every day after that horrific one, I made the decision not to tell, to carry the burden alone. I grossly underestimated the impact that unprovoked predicament would have on me, the damage it would cause for years to come.

Over those years though, the professional group had been a constant in my life, a backdrop to so many significant events. We celebrated weddings, mourned at funerals, welcomed new babies, and supported each other through breakups. Yet, when it came to my decision to step back and prioritize my mental health, it seemed like they couldn't be bothered to celebrate or even acknowledge the importance of my choice. It felt like they were breaking my heart all over again, for the last time.

In time, all the hurt, pain, and betrayals converged, overwhelming me completely. It was then that I understood I had reached rock bottom.

Though they were unreliable and untrustworthy at best, they were the closest I had to real friends. That made leaving the group feel like a difficult decision. But, it was necessary. I needed to focus on my healing, to give myself the space and time to process everything that had happened. It was a step towards reclaiming my life, towards finding peace and happiness on my own terms.

As I turned off the engine and stepped out of the car, I remember taking a deep breath, trying to steady myself.

I reminded myself that this was my journey. The evening of celebrating my new good news did not quite go as well as I had hoped, but it was all good. The path to healing was mine to walk, and while it was painful to leave behind those who couldn't support me, I knew it was the right choice. I was ready to embrace the future, to build a life that was truly my own, even if it meant doing it without the group that had once been so important to me.

As a final thought before I fell asleep that night, I asked myself, *"Can anyone see me?"*

Over the weeks, as I made my plans and saw them through unassisted, more than once, I questioned if anyone cared about me. Was it possible that no one else besides Momo actually loved me?

How can they give me distance when all I need is love?

CHAPTER EIGHT

ROCK BOTTOM

"Rock bottom became the solid foundation on which I rebuilt my life."
— *J.K. Rowling*

After getting settled, due to the obvious indifference shown by my people, there was no housewarming. I'm thinking maybe that's why the house is so cold all the time? The space is absolutely beautiful and extraordinarily peaceful but honestly, there is no joy inside.

I moved here with a refreshed perspective and a strong plan for rewiring my anxious mind. I researched and outlined ways and techniques to independently manage my stress. I was sure with the right environment and extreme reduction of distractions; I could heal myself by practicing mindfulness and engaging in calming hobbies like journaling and yoga.

Although the setting was perfect, reality soon took over and I developed a routine habit of just sleeping and crying to manage the tougher days. I was still too miserable to motivate myself.

The day I recognized the place I was in as "rock bottom" was the day true fear set in.

Typically, people tend to think that "hitting rock bottom" is reserved for abusers and addicts. Really, rock bottom is when a person feels they have reached the lowest of lows. You might feel emotionally overwhelmed, or broken, or worthless but everyone experiences their own version of rock bottom. So, the phrase "hitting rock bottom" differs for each individual.

For me, I was being hit by some of life's biggest waves with no recovery periods. The waves just kept coming, hitting me one after the other. Eventually, I flat-out hit rock bottom— emotionally, financially, mentally, and spiritually. The crash was painful in every way, and I finally had no choice but to face myself brutally, painfully, and honestly.

While plotting to just leave that messy chapter of my life behind, I initially felt a sense of relief, believing that distance alone would be enough to restore my mental well-being. However, three months into my lonely new life, I soon realized that simply changing my surroundings wasn't sufficient to reclaim my peace of mind. Running was not a resolution. The deeper work lay in transforming how I processed experiences and emotions. It became clear that healing required more than just a change of scenery; it demanded a profound shift in my mindset and the way I approached life's challenges.

As I bravely embarked on this journey, working closely with a local licensed therapist, I began to understand that many of the struggles I had perpetually faced in my adult years were rooted in my early years. Childhood traumas and the patterns I developed in response to them had followed me into adulthood, subtly influencing my reactions and decisions. Acknowledging this was the first step in a long process of healing. With proper coaching,

I also learned that healing is not a destination but an ongoing journey, requiring intentional effort and self-reflection. It involves peeling back layers of past experiences and truly understanding how they shape my present.

——————

As I pulled into the parking lot of the therapy center, I felt a familiar mix of anxiety and hope. The building was a modest two-story structure, nestled between a row of trees that provided a sense of privacy and calm. I parked my car and took a deep breath, trying to steady my racing thoughts. Therapy had been a lifeline for me, but the idea of confronting the past was daunting.

I made my way to the entrance and climbed the stairs to the second floor, each step echoing in the quiet stairwell. The waiting area was warm and inviting, with soft lighting and a collection of beautiful orchids that added a touch of elegance. The young, perfectly poised African American receptionist greeted me with a warm smile, her presence always a comforting start to my sessions.

"Good morning, Ms. Young," she said, checking me in. I nodded and took a seat, my eyes wandering over the room. The orchids were in full bloom, their vibrant colors a stark contrast to the turmoil I felt inside.

After a few moments, the door to the inner office opened, and my therapist, Dr. Collins, appeared. *"Ms. Young, I'm ready for you,"* she said with a gentle smile. I followed her into the therapy room, a space that had become a sanctuary for my thoughts and emotions.

Dr. Collins gestured for me to sit on the comfortable couch, and she settled into her chair across from me. We began with the usual niceties, discussing the week since our last session. But soon, the conversation turned to the nightmares that had been haunting me.

"I've been experiencing the nightmares again," I admitted, my voice barely above a whisper. *"They're so vivid, so terrifying. In them, Trevor is trying to kill me. I reported him to the police, and now he's hunting me down. At least three times each week, I wake up gasping, drenched in sweat, my heart pounding in my chest. The terror grips me so tightly I cannot breathe, cannot get back to sleep for hours, no matter how many times I try to tell myself that it was only a dream, that it wasn't real."*

Dr. Collins listened intently, her expression one of understanding and concern. *"Nightmares can be incredibly distressing,"* she said. *"Have you been able to use any of the coping techniques we've discussed?"*

I shook my head. *"I've tried, but my thoughts are racing, and I can't seem to reframe them or find any relief."*

We had worked on several coping techniques over the months. One was deep breathing exercises, where I focused on inhaling slowly through my nose and exhaling through my mouth, trying to calm my nervous system. Another was grounding, where I would focus on my surroundings, naming objects I could see, hear, and touch to bring myself back to the present moment. The third was journaling, a way to express my thoughts and feelings on paper, hoping to gain some clarity.

"In reality, I never talked about the incident," I confessed. *"I never reported him to the police. I never told anyone—not even my grandmother."*

Dr. Collins nodded, her eyes kind and reassuring. *"It's important to remember that talk therapy is a powerful tool,"* she said. *"It allows us to explore our thoughts and feelings in a safe environment. By talking about your experiences, we can work through them together and find a path to healing."*

I took a deep breath, feeling a little more grounded. *"Okay,"* I said. *"I'll start with what I can remember about the day leading up to the incident."*

I recounted the day, starting with leaving my grandmother's house around 11a.m. I stopped at Starbucks for my usual coffee fix, then headed to the nail salon for some much-needed self- care. Afterward, I went home, did a few chores with music playing in the background, and sat on the back patio, enjoying the view of the city. It was a peaceful afternoon, and I even managed to take a nap before getting ready for the 7:30p.m. meet-up with the professionals group.

"The meeting left me feeling a bit down," I continued. *"So, I called my friend, Trevor, and we agreed to meet at a local bar."*

Dr. Collins listened patiently, encouraging me to take my time. As I spoke, I could feel the weight of the past beginning to lift, if only slightly. The journey was far from over, but with each word, I was taking steps toward understanding and healing.

Practically in a trance, I continue to recount the events to Dr. Collins, my audience of one.

"It's the kind of morning that wraps around me like a fog, thick and dizzying. The sunlight filters through the thin curtains of my bedroom window, but the harsh light stings my eyes. I groan, pulling a pillow over my head, trying to drown out the pounding in my skull. My tongue is dry, and the taste of last night lingers on my lips—bitter and sour, unfamiliar.

I open my eyes again, squinting at the ceiling, trying to find some comfort in its familiar pattern, but it only makes my head spin more. I push myself up slowly, groaning as my body protests every movement. *"Where am I?"* My bedroom...yes. I'm in my bed. The blankets are twisted, and the sheets feel cold against my skin. A wet towel is touching me. I look over at my nightstand—my phone is missing. I feel the weight of confusion settle over me, like a fog I can't shake. *What happened?*

I stumble out of bed, my head still throbbing. I hold onto the wall for balance, making my way to the bathroom. My movements are slow, deliberate, as though my body is trying to figure out how to operate after the apparent chaos of the night before. The cool bathroom tile feels nice beneath my bare feet, and I take a breath, trying to calm the nausea rising in my throat.

Lounge. Bar. I *was* drinking, wasn't I? And Trevor— yes, Trevor was there too. But my mind is clouded with fog, with gaps where memories should be. I feel dizzy just thinking about it.

My clothes are strewn about—halfway in the closet, halfway out. I step toward the sink and look at myself in the mirror. My hair is tangled, sticking out at odd angles like a bird's nest. My makeup—if I had even bothered with it last night—is smeared, faint streaks of eyeliner and mascara marking my face.

The adrenalin is now surging as the urge to figure out what happened overwhelms me. I can't ignore the nagging questions anymore—*what did I do last night? What went wrong?* I stumble out of the bathroom and into the hallway, my body groaning with every step.

The hallway stretches out in front of me like a tunnel, its dark corners swallowed by shadows. Hanging on to the railing, I head downstairs. My feet shuffle across the floor as I near the living room.

The living room feels like a scene from a dream. The furniture looks askew, like it's been moved in a rush, but that doesn't make sense. I frown.

I lean against the wall for support, my eyes wandering to the kitchen. It looks eerily quiet, nothing out of place—except for the faint smell of vomit that still lingers in the air. My stomach churns again, and I grip the counter, afraid that any movement will trigger another wave of nausea.

My feet carry me toward the front door next. The foyer stretches out in front of me like a faint memory, my bare feet dragging as I reach the doorknob. I pause, catching my reflection in the mirror by the door. I look like I have been through hell. My gaze shifts toward the front porch, where the fresh daylight reveals what I recognize as Trevor's car parked in the driveway. My heart drops.

I swallow hard, and the memory begins to creep back in. Trevor's face. His hands on the wheel, the car swerving a little. I remember feeling dizzy, lightheaded. The sharp scent of his cologne, the way he was talking to me, trying to keep me awake. And then—my stomach revolting, the bile rising fast and— *"NO!"* I can't remember exactly how it happened, but I know it's there, the sensation of my body convulsing as I vomited in his car. For a split second, I had tried to hold it back, but my body betrayed me. I had ruined his car. I feel a wave of mortification.

My stomach churns, and I almost double over with the force of the memory. I stumble back inside, sinking onto the couch. My hands instinctively touch my face as I close my eyes. *"What did I do?"*

Bits and pieces of the night continue to creep into my mind. The conversations. The texting. The laughter. Trevor laughing, me laughing, but it's all mixed up with a sense of danger. The kind of danger that only comes when you can't remember your own actions. And then the car, the embarrassment, my attempt to escape the situation by running—but my body couldn't keep up. I **had** run, though, *hadn't I?*

My eyes flutter open, staring at the carpet beneath me, seeing nothing but the flash of fleeting images—the trash bin in the bathroom, Trevor's face, my own dread. The day ahead feels endless. I swallow again, forcing myself to stand up. I don't want to face Trevor, don't want to confront the mess I've made. But I have to. The events of last night aren't going anywhere. Neither is the sense of shame that clings to my skin like a second layer.

I take a deep breath, ready to face whatever comes next. I just hope Trevor can forgive me for what I've forgotten.

––––––––––

Overwhelmed by confusion and guilt, I resolve to contact Trevor, hoping to piece together the fragmented memories and apologize for the mess in his car. After hours of mustering the courage, I finally dial his number. The phone rings, and Trevor answers, his voice tinged with an unsettling tremor. *"What happened last night?"* I inquire; my voice barely steady.

"I'm sorry! I had too much to drink," Trevor says, abrupt and evasive, his voice shaky, almost too fast, as though he's trying to cover up something. The words hang in the air, thick and unsettling, but it's the way he says them that sends a cold shiver down my spine.

I blink, gripping the phone tighter. *"What?!"* His response feels... off. It doesn't make sense. It's not what I expected. I had assumed he would say something like, *"It's okay,"* or *"Don't worry about the car."* But instead, he sounds defensive—like he's trying to take the blame for something that he's not sure he should be taking the blame for.

I'm silent for a moment, the air in my house suddenly feeling too heavy, too still. My pulse quickens as the realization hits me: He's not telling the whole truth.

"Wait," I say, my voice shaking despite myself. *"What do you mean? What happened? I... I remember vomiting in your car, but I don't remember anything else. I don't even—**God**—I don't even remember how I got in the house."* My words spill out in a rush, the panic rising. The feeling of confusion in my chest is suffocating, and it's only getting worse.

There's a pause on the other end, a long stretch of silence that feels unbearable. It's almost like Trevor's weighing his next words, but when he speaks again, his voice is oddly tight, controlled. *"Look,"* he starts, *"I really don't want to talk about this right now."* The abruptness of his tone is like a slap in the face. *"It was just a messed-up night. I'm sorry if I made you uncomfortable. I—"* He cuts off, and the line goes quiet for a beat, and then he adds, *"I'll take care of the car, don't worry."*

His words are like empty promises, but it's the tone, that shaking quality in his voice, that sends a ripple of unease through me. Something about it feels like he's hiding something. I have so many questions, but all I can do is ask the one that's gnawing at me the most.

"No, Trevor," I say, the words coming out more forcefully than I expect, my voice rising with the pressure of the moment. *"What happened last night? You're acting like... like you're trying to avoid talking about it."*

There's another long pause, so long that I almost wonder if he's hung up. But when he finally speaks again, his voice is quieter, softer, but it still holds that same strange edge.

"I told you. I had too much to drink." He sighs heavily; a sound so heavy with regret that it almost breaks me. But there's still something *off* about him, something I can't quite place. *"Look, I'm sorry. I really am. I didn't mean for things to go the way they did. I don't want to hurt you. I just... I don't want to revisit it. Can we... can we just move past this?"*

Move past this?! I stare at the floor, my breath catching in my throat. I don't know what happened. I **need** to know what happened. How could he be so quick to dismiss it all?

"Move past this?" I repeat, my voice soft but tight with frustration. *"You're not even explaining anything. You've barely said anything about what actually happened. I—I can't just let it go like this."* I feel my chest tighten with both fear and anger. *"I'm really sorry, Trevor, but you can't just say that and expect me to be okay with it."*

There's a sharp intake of breath from his side of the phone, and then—silence again. The kind of silence that's more telling than anything else he could say. And just as I'm about to say something, anything to press for more, Trevor's voice cracks in a way that makes my stomach drop.

"Please don't be mad at me," he whispers. *"I—I just... I don't know what to say."*

My heart lurches. The vulnerability in his voice, the way his words almost break apart, is both unexpected and disorienting. But still, it doesn't explain the strange distance between us, the oddness of the conversation, the discomfort that now sits like an unshakable weight between us.

I feel my own frustration bubble up, the question pushing past my lips before I can stop it. *"Trevor... were we okay last night? Did something happen?"* My voice falters on the last part, but I can't help it. The fear, the need to know the truth, it's too much.

The answer I get is nothing like what I expect.

"No," Trevor says quietly, so quietly that I almost don't hear him, *"nothing happened. Nothing bad, I mean. I... I just don't remember everything either. I don't know what to tell you, okay?"* His voice cracks again, but this time, there's no apology in it, just something raw—almost panicked.

My mind races, trying to put all the pieces together, trying to understand what he's saying, trying to understand *why* he won't just tell me. The truth hangs in the air between us, elusive and frightening, and the more he withholds, the deeper the unease sinks into my bones.

"I have to go," Trevor says suddenly, his voice sounding tight and panicked. *"I—I'll talk to you later."*

Before I can say anything else, he hangs up. The line goes dead. And for a moment, I stand there in the quiet, the phone still pressed to my ear, my mind shattered from the unanswered questions, from the words he *didn't* say.

Something isn't right, something about his voice, about his refusal to tell me what happened. I feel a gnawing unease settle deep within me, and despite every part of me telling me to drop it, I know I can't. I have to find out what exactly happened last night, no matter how long it takes, no matter how much it hurts—because Trevor's words didn't answer my questions; they only raised more.

Reeling from the growing sense of unease, I made my way back upstairs to scrutinize the bedroom more closely. At first glance, everything appeared normal, except for a damp towel carelessly tossed on the bed. I vaguely recalled taking a shower the previous night, but the details were hazy. As I stepped back into the bathroom, a sudden realization struck me with the force of a ton of bricks...

It's not the mess that catches my attention—it's the trash can beside the toilet. A used condom is hanging out close to the top, partially wrapped in tissue. I pause, the sight of it making my stomach lurch.

My eyes flick to the contents deeper inside the bin, and I notice something else that shouldn't be there. My heart skips a beat as I kneel closer. A second used condom.

CHAPTER NINE

CLARITY

"Out of suffering have emerged the strongest souls; the most massive characters are seared with scars."
— Khalil Gibran

In the weeks following that therapy session about Trevor, I began to notice subtle yet profound changes in my life. The nightmares that had haunted my nights for years started to dissipate, like fog lifting after a storm. Gradually, week after week, the dreams became fewer and farther between. When they did come, they were less vivid, less suffocating. The images weren't as sharp or as intrusive. It was as if the act of speaking my truth had pulled the weight off my chest and allowed my mind to rest. No longer was I trapped in the cycle of terror that replayed the trauma over and over again. The shadows that had loomed over my subconscious were finally being illuminated by the light of understanding and acceptance.

Healing didn't happen instantly, nor did I wake up one day suddenly free of the weight I'd carried for so long. However, shortly after that life-changing emotional leap from the comfort of a therapy couch, I definitely felt a sense of *release*, as if something deep inside me had unlocked. And for that, I was incredibly grateful.

And the guilt—*the guilt*—ceased.

In the aftermath of the assault, the weight of guilt and shame had become an unbearable burden. In the first two months, I lost over 20 pounds—a significant amount for someone who didn't have much to spare. My body was in a constant state of stress, and I was barely eating or sleeping. The emotional turmoil manifested physically, and I felt like I was withering away.

I had blamed myself. I thought, deep down, that it was somehow my fault. I thought that maybe I had done something, said something, or acted in a way that invited this upon me. I had spent countless nights trying to figure out what went wrong, playing the evening over and over in my head, picking apart every detail, every interaction with Trevor, searching for the moment I could pinpoint as the one where everything had unraveled.

Around the third month, I experienced something that I later learned was my very first panic attack. It started with a light pain in my chest, which quickly escalated into a sharp, stabbing sensation. I felt like I couldn't draw a full breath, as if my lungs were refusing to cooperate. The fear was overwhelming, and I was convinced something was seriously wrong. In a state of panic, I drove myself to the emergency room. The medical staff ran tests, administered morphine, and kept me under observation for two days. During that time, I finally slept—truly slept—for the first time in months. My absence from work went unnoticed until my colleagues, concerned by my no call no shows, tracked me down at the hospital.

The experience was a wake-up call, but it also deepened my isolation. For years, I couldn't bring myself to trust anyone. The fear of being judged or blamed for what happened kept me silent.

I was trapped in a cycle of self-blame and shame, too embarrassed to share my story. The stigma surrounding assault and the fear of victim-blaming were powerful deterrents, keeping me from seeking the help I desperately needed.

The damage from carrying this guilt was profound. It affected my relationships, my work, and my overall well-being. I was constantly on edge, always waiting for the other shoe to drop.

The emotional scars were deep, and the journey to healing felt insurmountable. By this point, all of my stressors had come together—work pressures, toxic relationships, unresolved trauma, and the relentless self-blame. Each one weighed heavily on me, but when they all collided at once, it felt like the perfect storm. The overwhelming burden became too much to bear, and I found myself figuratively standing on the edge, questioning if I could continue at all.

For as long as I could remember, my body had been a source of discomfort—a place I wanted to escape from, a prison I couldn't stand to be in. I hated looking in the mirror. I hated how foreign I felt in my own skin, how the touch of fabric against my body could feel like an invasion. I avoided touch altogether—hugs, handshakes, anything that made me feel exposed, vulnerable. I had become a shell, hollowed out, trying desperately to avoid being seen.

Acknowledging the impact of these experiences was my first step toward recovery. Talking about my pain in therapy, with a licensed professional who had the training and the knowledge to help me unpack my emotions, helped me understand something I hadn't realized before: I had been carrying an unjust burden, and I didn't have to. The guilt I felt was not mine to own.

No one tells you how long it takes to undo the damage done by years of self-blame, especially when society often whispers the lie that you should have done something differently. But working with Dr. Collins, I began to piece together the truth: The assault was not my fault. The way I responded to it wasn't my fault and I didn't have to live with the crushing weight of guilt anymore. It was as though the burden had been taken off my shoulders and placed where it belonged—with the person who had hurt me. The weight of that guilt—of carrying responsibility for something that was never mine to bear—began to lift.

All things considered, one of the most transformative realizations was that I was not at fault for the assault. This understanding was both liberating and empowering. It allowed me to shed the suffocating skin of self-blame and step into a new identity—one where I felt seen and understood, rather than embarrassed or ashamed. Sharing my story became easier, not just with Dr. Collins, but with others who had walked similar paths. I discovered a community of support and solidarity, where my experiences were validated, and my voice was heard.

It was only through self-love, patience, and eventually reaching out for support that I began to find my way back to myself.

———

Finally opening up about that night felt like releasing a breath I didn't know I was holding. For years, the weight of that secret had pressed down on me, casting shadows over my days and haunting my nights with relentless nightmares. So, as the words tumbled out, I felt a strange mix of vulnerability and liberation. It was as if I had been carrying a heavy backpack up a steep hill, and now, at last, I could set it down. The relief was palpable, a soothing balm on the raw edges of my mind, and I could feel the beginning of a lightness I hadn't experienced in years.

It was addicting.

I continued my weekly sessions with Dr. Collins, and with each session, I felt a little more at peace, a little more in control of my own narrative.

Although I had tried talk therapy over the phone before, working with Dr. Collins was a pivotal step in my healing journey. She provided a safe space where I could confront the past without fear of judgment or misunderstanding. She helped me unravel the tangled web of emotions and memories that had kept me ensnared in a cycle of guilt and shame. Through the cognitive-behavioral techniques and trauma-focused therapy, I learned to reframe my thoughts and challenge the negative beliefs that had taken root in my mind. In time, the personal guilt that had weighed so heavily on my shoulders began to lift, replaced by a growing sense of self-compassion and forgiveness.

Another profound realization that blessed me is that the journey of healing is not a linear path, nor is it a "one and done" approach. It is a winding road, filled with unexpected turns and challenges. It requires ongoing effort and commitment to maintain mental and emotional well-being. Childhood traumas and past experiences can leave deep imprints on our psyche, influencing our thoughts and behaviors well into adulthood.

Recognizing this, I understood that healing is a continuous process, one that involves nurturing my mental health with the same care and attention I would give to any other aspect of my life. Dr. Collins emphasized that every step forward is a testament to personal growth and resilience, a reminder that *I have the strength* to overcome the scars of my past.

One evening, as I sat on the comfortable couch, the soft hum of the air conditioner providing a gentle backdrop to our sessions, I realized and acknowledged that while I had made significant strides in overcoming the trauma of the assault, there were other shadows lurking in the corners of my mind. These shadows were not as immediately apparent as the ones cast by Trevor's actions, but they were just as insidious, creeping into my daily life and affecting my professional world.

For over a decade, I had navigated a career path littered with obstacles that seemed to echo the dysfunction of my past. Incompetent supervisors who promised promotions that never materialized, colleagues who took credit for my work, and leaders who marginalized my contributions—all these experiences had left me feeling undervalued and invisible. It was as if I was trapped in a cycle of professional purgatory, unable to break free from the patterns that had been established in my childhood.

Growing up, I was the peacemaker in my family, always striving to earn the approval of my parents and siblings. This role had taught me to prioritize others' needs over my own, a habit that had seeped into my professional life. I found it difficult to set boundaries, fearing that doing so would lead to conflict or, worse, rejection. This fear was a constant companion, whispering in my ear that I was not enough, that I had to keep proving my worth to be accepted.

In therapy, I began to unravel these threads, tracing them back to their origins. Dr. Collins, a patient and insightful guide, helped me see that my inability to set boundaries was not a personal failing but a learned behavior. It was a survival mechanism that had served me in my youth but was now holding me back. She encouraged me to practice assertiveness, to voice my needs and expectations clearly and without apology.

The first time I tried this at work, my heart pounded in my chest like a drum. I was in a meeting with my supervisor, a man who had a knack for making me feel small with his dismissive comments and condescending tone. As he began to outline yet another project that would stretch my already thin resources, I took a deep breath and spoke up.

"I appreciate the opportunity to take on new challenges," I said, my voice steady despite the anxiety swirling inside me. *"However, I need to ensure that my current workload is manageable before I can commit to additional responsibilities."*

The room fell silent, and for a moment, I feared I had overstepped. But then, to my surprise, my supervisor nodded, acknowledging my concerns. It was a small victory, but a significant one. It marked the beginning of a shift in how I approached my work and my relationships within it.

As I continued to practice setting boundaries, I noticed changes not only in how others treated me but also in how I viewed myself. I began to see my worth not as something to be earned through endless sacrifice but as an inherent part of who I was. This realization was liberating, allowing me to step out of the shadows of my past and into the light of a future where I could advocate for myself with confidence.

Of course, the journey was not without setbacks. There were days when the old patterns reasserted themselves, when I found myself slipping back into the role of the accommodating peacemaker. But each time this happened, I reminded myself that healing is not a straight line. It is a series of steps forward and backward, a dance that requires patience and perseverance.

In the end, I came to understand that the injustices I faced in my professional life were not solely the result of external forces but were also tied to the internal barriers I had erected over the years. By dismantling these barriers, I was able to create a space where I could thrive, both personally and professionally.

The journey of healing is ongoing, a lifelong commitment to nurturing my mental and emotional well-being. But with each step I take, I move closer to a place of peace and fulfillment, where the shadows of the past no longer dictate the course of my future.

Seeking help from a professional was one of the most courageous decisions I ever made, and I encourage anyone who has experienced trauma to consider doing the same. Healing is possible, but it requires intentional effort and a willingness to confront the past. As I continue on this journey, I am reminded that while the work is challenging, it is also profoundly rewarding.

Each step forward is a testament to my resilience and a reminder that I am not alone. The path to healing is ongoing, but with each day, I grow stronger and more whole.

———————

It's late, much later than I expected. The air is heavy with the chill that comes with the night, but I welcome it. As the sun dipped below the horizon, casting a warm, golden hue over the Chattanooga skyline, I found myself once again on my back patio, a place that had become both a sanctuary and a stage for my deepest reflections. Out here, I can finally breathe and feel the weight of the world lift—just a little. The air was thick with the scent of honeysuckle, a sweet reminder of the summers spent with my grandmother, whose love had been the only constant in my tumultuous life. Tonight, however, the sweetness was tinged with a bitterness that I couldn't quite shake off.

The house behind me is quiet, my mind far from it. Inside, I could almost hear the voices of my old friends, the ones I invited to my birthday celebration. I could almost hear the *no's* piling up in my mind, each refusal cutting deeper than the last.

Cheddar lay sprawled at my feet, her soft, rhythmic breathing a soothing balm to my frayed nerves. The feeling of her, the weight of her affection, is the only thing that keeps me grounded right now. I never thought I could love something the way I love her. In her eyes, I see unconditional loyalty. A loyalty I've never been able to offer myself, and yet, she gives it to me freely. I don't deserve it. But somehow, she thinks I do.

She had been my lifeline, my reason to get up each morning when the weight of the world threatened to crush me. Adopting her had been a desperate attempt to find meaning, a last-ditch effort to tether myself to this world when I felt like I was slipping away. Little did I know that this golden retriever, with her boundless energy and unconditional love, would become my anchor.

She came into my life when I thought it was too late to care about anything. When the thought of another day felt like an endless climb up a mountain too high to ever conquer. I had hit rock bottom long before I even realized I was there. The grief from losing my grandmother had almost suffocated me. She was the only person who ever loved me fully. After she passed, it felt like the last bit of love I would ever receive disappeared with her. The loneliness became deafening, and my own mind, the very thing I thought I could rely on, turned into an endless echo chamber of doubt, resentment, and anger.

But then, Cheddar showed up. A refuge in a time of storm. When I adopted her, I had nothing left. I couldn't even tell you why I thought bringing an animal into my life was the answer. I guess I needed someone who would love me in a way that didn't demand anything of me. No questions. No conditions. She didn't need me to be anything but myself. And she was there, through every low, every panic attack, every moment I wanted to let go. Cheddar saved me, in ways I still don't think I fully understand.

I let out a deep breath and gaze at the stars above, distant and indifferent. The night seems to be holding me, as though it's trying to remind me that life is still worth living, even when it's hard. Even when it feels pointless. I close my eyes, and for a moment, I feel the warmth of Cheddar's fur against me, the steady rhythm of her breath.

"Come here, girl," I whisper, and Cheddar stands. She lays her head in my lap, eyes shining with that quiet, trusting gaze.

I run my fingers through her thick coat, letting the calm settle over me. For the first time tonight, my breath feels even, steady.

As I sit here, the memories of my 40th birthday party— *or rather, the lack thereof*—played on a loop in my mind. I had envisioned a celebration of healing, a testament to the hard work I had put into reclaiming my mental health. But the empty house and the silence that greeted me today were a stark reminder that not everyone was willing to walk this path with me. It was a devastating blow, one that left me questioning the very foundation of my progress.

That's the lie we tell ourselves, isn't it? That once we heal, everything will fall into place.

I invited them. I opened myself up, made myself vulnerable, and they declined. Every single one of them. And tonight, it feels like that rejection has brought me right back to the edge, to that place where my mind still whispers about giving up, about surrendering.

But then I feel Cheddar nudge my hand with her cold nose, reminding me that there's still something worth fighting for. Not just her, but *me*.

I've worked too hard for this. Too hard to give up now.

As I sit here, the realization settles in. There's so much I still don't understand, but I've definitely learned one thing: mental health doesn't come with a destination. It's not a place you arrive at, like crossing the finish line of a race. It's more like running a marathon that never ends. I've learned to take things one step at a time, even when the road is rocky, even when the pain feels like it might swallow me whole.

The world doesn't owe me anything, and I've finally learned that I don't owe anyone anything either. Not in the way I thought I did. All my life, I'd been trying to please others, trying to live up to their expectations. But now, I realize the most important thing I can do is honor myself. To listen to my own needs. To take care of my own heart.

Yet, as the night deepened and the stars began to twinkle above, I felt a shift within me. It was subtle, like the first hint of dawn after a long, dark night. I realized that the journey I was on was mine alone, and that the validation I sought from others was a mirage, an illusion that had kept me trapped in a cycle of self-doubt and despair.

I sit here on this patio, with Cheddar curled up beside me, and I let go of the need for validation. The party that never happened, the empty RSVPs, the people who don't see me—they don't define me anymore.

"Now, I'm allowing myself to acknowledge that the praise and honor are my personal responsibility," I whisper into the quiet night, the words ringing in my ears. *"I set goals that motivate me. I aim to achieve certain objectives because they are important to me. It's always imperative that I see value in the things that I strive for, so why then does it matter if someone else recognizes my hard work and*

dedication? Tonight, I finally acknowledge that it doesn't matter, and it never did."

Cheddar's soft breathing matches mine. I can feel the love radiating from her, a steady current, and I think about how much she's helped me. She's always been there, even when I thought I was too broken to be loved. Just her presence makes me believe that maybe, just maybe, I'm not too broken after all. In her presence, I found a sense of peace that had eluded me for so long. Medical studies have shown that caring for an animal can significantly improve mental health, reducing stress and anxiety, and providing a sense of purpose. Cheddar was living proof of that. She had taught me the value of living in the moment, of finding joy in the simple act of being.

But I had to understand that it was okay to be sad, to feel disappointed. What mattered was not staying in that place, not allowing those feelings to define me. I had to learn to be vigilant, to recognize the signs of my mental speed bumps, and to navigate them with grace and resilience.

As the night wore on, I felt a sense of calm washing over me. I was not alone, not truly. I had Cheddar, and I had myself. And that was enough. I chose to celebrate my progress; to honor the work I had done to reclaim my life. It was a quiet celebration, one that needed no audience, no applause. It was a testament to the strength I had found within myself, a strength that had been there all along, waiting to be discovered.

In the stillness of the night, I make a vow to continue this journey, to embrace the challenges and the triumphs with equal measure. I will not let the shadows of my past dictate my future. I choose to live. I choose to move forward. I choose to be kind to myself, even when I don't feel like it. The sadness might return tomorrow, or the day after. That's just how it goes. But for tonight, I'm going to enjoy this moment. And I know, deep down, that even on the hardest nights, I don't have to face this alone. Cheddar is here, and she's the most faithful companion I could ask for.

The night stretches on, quiet and peaceful, and for the first time in a long while, I feel a flicker of hope. It's small, almost imperceptible, but it's there. And that's enough. That's more than enough.

As I sit here, under the vast expanse of the Tennessee sky, grateful for my life, I know that I am exactly where I need to be. I am home.

EPILOGUE

STANDING STRONG

*"You may encounter many defeats, but you must not be defeated.
In fact, it may be necessary to encounter the defeats, so you can
know who you are, what you can rise from, how you can still
come out of it."*
— Maya Angelou

Sometimes, I wonder how different life would have been if I'd had the chance to fully live. Instead of dedicating so much time to healing from wounds that were never my fault. If only I had been able to put down the weight of trauma and truly savor the freedom of simply existing, without the constant pressure of surviving. But life doesn't always give us that luxury. Some of us are handed burdens we never asked for, and instead of having the chance to just be, we spend our days rebuilding ourselves, piece by broken piece.

After twelve years, I finally contacted Trevor. Yes, the same Trevor. The one who assaulted me that night, the one whose face I still saw every time I closed my eyes. I'll admit, there was a part of me that didn't want to reach out. My first instinct was to hold onto the idea that he was just another person who would never see me for who I really was, or at least who I was becoming. But I had made a commitment to myself. Healing was not just about addressing the wounds caused by others; it was about being whole in spite of them. I needed to take this final step, even if it would hurt.

Reaching out to Trevor was one of the hardest things I've ever done. With the guidance and support of Dr. Collins, I finally mustered the courage to confront the man who had caused me so much pain. I learned how to push through the fear and the anger. Therapy had been a long, painful process, but it was necessary. You can only grow when you confront the things you've been avoiding. And so, I dialed the number and waited for him to pick up, my heart pounding in my chest.

"Hello?" His voice, so familiar yet foreign, made me freeze for a moment.

"Trevor," I started, my voice shaky at first, but growing steadier with each word, *"I wanted to talk to you about what happened twelve years ago. I need you to hear me out."*

He was quick to respond, and the dismissiveness in his tone was instant. *"Oh, that? Yeah, I didn't think it was that big of a deal. I thought you wanted it. You were into me, right?"*

That was the moment I realized he had a completely different recollection of that night. His memory was warped, twisted into something that made him the hero in his own mind, while I was just some passive participant. I could feel the rage bubbling up in my chest, but I took a deep breath, reminding myself that this wasn't about him—it was about me.

"No, Trevor. I didn't want that. I didn't ask for it. I was unconscious, for God's sake. I was a victim. You were the one who drugged me and took advantage of me, and you're basically still doing it by pretending it was something I consented to."

128

He paused. For a moment, there was silence on the other end of the line, as if he couldn't quite process what I was saying. When he finally spoke again, it was almost dismissive, as if he couldn't be bothered to even acknowledge the pain he had caused. *"I didn't know you felt that way. I'm sorry, I guess. But it's in the past, right? I didn't mean to hurt you. I don't think I did."*

His denial and fabricated memory were infuriating, but not surprising. What stung the most was his complete oblivion to the damage he had caused, the mental trauma that had haunted me for years. How dare he live his life, untouched by the consequences of his actions, while I teetered on the edge, struggling to find my footing? The words hit me like a slap in the face, harder than any physical blow.

How in the hell can he act like none of this mattered to him? Twelve years, a lifetime of trauma, and he had been walking around all this time completely oblivious. He had walked all the way home, then, clumsily apologized to me the very next morning so HOW was that possible? How could he continue on with his life, unscathed, while I was left picking up the shattered pieces of mine?

My mind raced.

I felt a wave of frustration and anger, but then something unexpected happened. A sense of peace began to wash over me. Not because he apologized or took accountability—*he didn't*—but because I had finally found my voice. I had finally confronted the past, not for him, but for me. I did it. I had taken control of that situation, even if I didn't get the closure I thought I needed. I realized that the peace I sought would never come from him. It could only come from within.

And in that moment, I felt lighter. For the first time in twelve years, I wasn't carrying that weight anymore. I could breathe.

"Take care, Trevor."

In my professional life, I have learned the hard way that respect is non-negotiable. I don't care if you're a supervisor, an advisor, a sun visor, or a Budweiser—*you're going to talk to me and treat me like you got some sense.* All I cared about was being treated with respect. That was the truth. The time for pretending I was okay with being treated like less than, was over. No more. No more putting up with condescending behavior, toxic environments, or people who thought they could push me around because I wasn't firm enough to set boundaries. Those days were over.

That is why after years of turning the other cheek, I took the legal route with my former employer. I had spent way too much time in a hostile work environment, dealing with harassment and retaliation from colleagues and management. I had been silenced for far too long, afraid to speak up because of the pressure to conform to the workplace "culture." So, after enduring years of unfair treatment—being undermined, belittled, and held back, I finally took a stand and sued the company for hostile workplace, harassment, discrimination, and retaliation. The case was a long battle, filled with late nights, sleepless moments, and additional perpetual stress that also nearly pushed me to the brink.

In the end, I won. A $289,000 settlement, along with a promotion and back pay for the six years preceding the case. While it wasn't a fortune, it was a victory—one that sent a clear message to my former employer and anyone else who thought they could take advantage of me. And still, as I reflected on the fight, I couldn't help but feel a sense of indignation. Those who stood by and watched me struggle, who didn't understand the weight of what I was going through, had no clue what it felt like to fight for something you deserve.

The victory was also a stark reminder of the struggles I had faced. From cradle to grave, it was easy for those not in my shoes to misunderstand my situation, to dismiss my experiences as mere oversensitivity. But I know the truth. I am accountable for my own actions, for my tendency to people-please and my failure to set clear and firm boundaries early on. I get that. However, those who chose to misunderstand my challenges also chose to ignore the broader implications of such injustices.

As Dr. Martin Luther King Jr. said, *"Injustice anywhere is a threat to justice everywhere."* I have spent years advocating for myself and others, often fighting necessary battles alone. With the intensity and brazenness of callous behaviors and hatred elevating each day, I fear that our nation will soon face a reckoning, a battle that no one can ignore or escape. But I can rest knowing that I did my part, that I stood up for what was right.

Throughout my case, as I reflected on my progress, I thought about how often people turned their backs on me, often with no explanation. How easy it was for them to judge from the outside, to claim I was simply naive, or to think I was too emotional. But they didn't know. They didn't know what it was like to navigate a world that was not designed for people like me. They didn't understand the complexities of dealing with both racial and gender-based barriers in a career that wasn't built for people from my background, for people with my quirks. And yet, I persevered. I fought for myself, and I fought for others who were still waiting for their turn to be heard.

While I was the face in this case, this was not just my battle; this was the battle of anyone who has ever been silenced, overlooked, or mistreated. It was a battle for fairness, for dignity, for respect.

For too long, people like me have been told to *"just deal with it"* or *"suck it up,"* but I realized that we are not defined by the things that happen to us, but by how we rise in the face of them.

———

Healing is a journey, one that requires patience and self-compassion. Nobody really talks about the exhaustion that comes with healing past traumas. Once your body comes out of "fight or flight" mode, it craves rest and silence. It's not laziness; it's your body catching up on years of unrest. You deserve this peace. Now, as I sit here, I feel a calm that I've never experienced before.

It's the stillness that comes from healing, the kind of peace that your body desires after years of being in "survival" mode. My body finally feels safe. After years of constantly being on guard, it's as though my soul has finally been allowed to rest. I'm no longer fighting battles that aren't mine. I'm no longer afraid of what the future holds. I have faith that God will protect me through whatever comes next, just as He always has.

bell hooks once said, *"One of the best guides to how to be self-loving is to give ourselves the love we are often dreaming about receiving from others."* For so long, I had looked for validation from the wrong places— whether from people who didn't deserve it, or from situations that only served to hurt me. But now, I have learned to give myself that love. Outside of God, I am my own source of peace, my own protector, and my own advocate.

I've come to realize, the purpose of life is love and joy —not to ruin either of those for others through our words, thoughts, or actions. My journey has taught me that peace doesn't come from external validation; it comes from within. Philippians 4:7 reminds us, *"And the peace of God, which transcends all understanding, will guard your hearts and your minds in*

Christ Jesus." That peace is something I've finally come to embrace.

I'm no longer afraid of the world, or the people who would try to tear me down. And I refuse to allow anyone to rob me of the joy I've worked so hard to find.

And now, as I look back on everything—everything I've been through, the pain and the triumphs, the brokenness and the healing—I know that I am stronger than I ever realized. The battles I've fought weren't just for me. They were for every person who has been told they aren't enough, for every person who has been silenced, for every person who has been made to feel small. I've fought so we can all stand tall.

And so, as I close this chapter, I know that my journey isn't over. It's just beginning. But I'm ready now. Ready to face the world with peace in my heart, and strength in my soul. Because, in the end, I've learned that the peace I was searching for was always within me. I just had to be brave enough to claim it.

www.ingramcontent.com/pod-product-compliance
Lightning Source LLC
Chambersburg PA
CBHW020659260626
47157CB00008B/3102